THIS BOOK
~~BELONGS TO~~:
acquired by:

____

Ba

BANDETTE

NDETTE™

in The Six Finger Secret

Story by PAUL TOBIN

Art by COLLEEN COOVER

DARK HORSE BOOKS

President and Publisher MIKE RICHARDSON
Editor SHANTEL LAROCQUE
Associate Editor BRETT ISRAEL
Designer KATHLEEN BARNETT
Digital Art Technician CHRISTINA MCKENZIE and ANN GRAY

This volume collects issues fourteen through eighteen of the Monkeybrain comic book series *Bandette*.

ChickenBasket © Font Diner
www.fontdiner.com

Published by Dark Horse Books
A division of Dark Horse Comics LLC
10956 SE Main Street
Milwaukie, Oregon 97222

DarkHorse.com

Library of Congress Cataloging-in-Publication Data

Names: Tobin, Paul, 1965- author. | Coover, Colleen, artist.
Title: The six finger secret / story by Paul Tobin ; art by Colleen Coover.

Description: First edition. | Milwaukie, OR : Dark Horse Books, 2021. | Series: Bandette ; volume 4 | "This volume collects issues fourteen through eighteen of the Monkeybrain comic book series Bandette" | Audience: Ages 14+ | Summary: "The most unlikely of patrons hires Bandette, the greatest thief in the world, to pilfer a painting whose brushstrokes hold centuries of hidden messages. Unfortunately, a series of felonious rivals contrive to snatch the art for themselves!"– Provided by publisher.
Identifiers: LCCN 2020009254 | ISBN 9781506719269 (hardcover)
Subjects: LCSH: Graphic novels. | CYAC: Graphic novels. | Robbers and outlaws–Fiction. | Art thefts–Fiction.
Classification: LCC PZ7.7.T62 Si 2021 | DDC 741.5/973–dc23
LC record available at https://lccn.loc.gov/2020009254

First edition: July 2021
Hardcover ISBN: 978-1-50671-926-9

10 9 8 7 6 5 4 3 2 1
Printed in China

Previously...

BANDETTE, the greatest thief in the world, has THRILLED us with her MANY EXCITING ADVENTURES!

She has THWARTED the plans of ABSINTHE and his criminal organization, FINIS!

She has FACED DOWN the fatal threat of the deadly strangler, IL TREDICI!

She has RUN AFOUL of the shadowy underworld figure known only as THE VOICE!

She has LOCKED HORNS with the crossbow-wielding villainess, DART PETITE!

She has MATCHED WITS with her most talented rival in thievery, MONSIEUR!

She has TRADED BLOWS and SHOPPING ADVICE with her mortal foe and good friend, MATADORI!

She has been a source of PAINFUL HEARTBURN in the breast of POLICE INSPECTOR B.D. BELGIQUE!

What further adventures await!?

And now, MORE BANDETTE!

CHAPTER ONE

£#%ø*!!

TREMBLE
TREMBLE

ME? REDUCED TO THIS?
IT'S INSANITY! IT'S UNBEFITTING A POLICEMAN!
IT'S Σ#$%.!!
PURE %ø#¡&.!!

IT'S THE SMARTEST THING TO DO AND YOU KNOW IT.
WHEN YOU NEED HELP, CALL AN EXPERT.

¶¡*@&.

PUFF
PUFF
PUFF

CRASH!
¡#β%ø*!!
KICK!

POP!
π#@÷%!!
FLING!

HMPFF.
GRAB!

ELSEWHERE...
I DIDN'T EXPECT YOU TO ARRIVE SO SOON!
THIS IS SO EXCITING! I'VE HEARD SO MUCH ABOUT YOU!
BUT OF COURSE WE SHOULD TALK BUSINESS.
THERE IS... A PAINTING I NEED TO HAVE...ACQUIRED. A PAINTING BY PIERRE SUBLEYRAS.

SUBLEYRAS? A TALENTED PAINTER, MADAME ROCHLAW, BUT...HARDLY WORTH THE TIME OF A MAN OF MY TALENTS.
PERHAPS YOU SHOULD FIND A MORE COMMONPLACE THIEF WHO...?
I CAN PAY YOU! HERE! LOOK!

A TIDY SUM. BUT A BORING ONE. I AM MUCH MORE THAN A MERE THIEF. I AM AN ARTIST.
THERE IS NO ROMANCE TO THIS THEFT. NO SPICE. NO ALLURE.

AGAIN, I BELIEVE YOU WOULD BE BEST SERVED BY A BURGLAR, RATHER THAN...
YOU WANT ALLURE? SPICE?

THEN COME INSIDE, AND I WILL TELL YOU A TALE THAT IS AT TIMES SCANDALOUS, AND AT OTHER TIMES BLOODY.
I WILL TELL YOU ALL ABOUT THE LONG AND STORIED HISTORY OF THE PAINTING KNOWN AS... THE SIX FINGER SECRET.

TELL ME.

ELSEWHERE...
SO YOU'RE THE FEMME FELON, EH?
FAIR ENOUGH. YOU LOOK TRUSTWORTHY. OR RATHER, YOU DON'T.
AND THAT THERE'S THE WHOLE POINT, BECAUSE AT THE REQUEST OF MY BOSS I NEED YOU TO STEAL A PAINTING.

IT'S KNOWN AS "THE ARTIST'S STUDIO."
THE ORIGINAL PAINTER WAS PIERRE SUBLEYRAS, BUT, WELL, THERE'S BEEN A BUNCHA OTHER ARTISTS... BOTH GOOD N' BAD... WHO WORKED ON THE CANVAS AFTER THAT SUBLEYRAS GUY.
HERE, I CAN BEST EXPLAIN BY SHOWING YOU...

...THIS ROUGH COPY OF THE PAINTING.

ELSEWHERE...

SO, NNNN, LET ME GET THIS STRAIGHT.
THIS PICTURE WAS, NNNN, COMMISSIONED BY MADAME DE POMPADOUR, WHO WAS SOME SORT OF...HARLOT, YOU SAY?
A COURTESAN, NOT A HARLOT, BUT...YES.

MADAME DE POMPADOUR USED THE PAINTING AS A MEANS OF SECRET COMMUNICATION WITH HER MORE...
...ILLICIT LOVERS.

THE ORIGINAL PAINTING WAS CREATED BY SUBLEYRAS...
BUT MADAME DE POMPADOUR HAD TWO STAFF ARTISTS REWORKING IT ON AN ALMOST DAILY BASIS...
...CONSTANTLY INSERTING NEW VIGNETTES INTO THE PAINTINGS WITHIN THE COMPOSITION--VISUAL MESSAGES ONLY HER ADMIRERS COULD UNDERSTAND.
MEANING THEY COULD EASILY "READ" THESE PRIVATE MESSAGES IN PUBLIC.

ELSEWHERE...
AHH, I SEE WHAT YOU MEAN. HOW THRILLING!
WHEN TWO LOVERS CONDUCT THEIR PRIVATE BUSINESS IN PUBLIC, PASSING NOTES, WE CAN FEEL THE THRILL AND THE THRUM OF OUR HEARTS BEATING IN OUR CHESTS, NO?

UMM, YES. ERR, TO THE POINT...
...LONG AFTER THE TIME OF MADAME DE POMPADOUR HAD PASSED, THE P-PAINTING CONTINUED TO BE USED FOR THESE PURPOSES.
P-PASSING N-NOTES, I MEAN.

"IT WAS USED BY NAPOLEON'S SPIES TO FERRY INFORMATION B-BACK AND FORTH..."
OH, WASN'T THIS IN THE EAST GALLERY LAST WEEK?
"THE NOBILITY NEVER KNEW THE P-PAINTING THEY ADMIRED WAS INFORMING NAPOLEON ABOUT THEIR DEEPEST SECRETS."

"IT WAS USED BY TOULOUSE LAUTREC TO CONTACT HIS MISTRESSES. OR AT LEAST, THOSE MISTRESSES HE DIDN'T WANT HIS MOTHER TO KNOW ABOUT."
AGAIN, LIVI? WHAT IS IT WITH YOU?
EVERY MORNING WE COME TO THIS DINGY CAFÉ AND YOU JUST STARE AT THAT PAINTING ALL DREAMY-EYED AND GIGGLING.

"IT WAS USED BY CHARLES DE GAULLE DURING THE WAR, PASSING MESSAGES TO THE RESISTANCE."
THE TREE MUST HAVE SIX LANTERNS, ONLY THREE OF THEM LIT.
HURRY, WE MUST RE-HANG THE PAINTING IN THE OLD CHURCH BEFORE NIGHTFALL.

ALL VERY INTERESTING, YOU HANDSOME MAN. BUT WHY HAVE YOU APPROACHED ME?
WHAT DOES SUCH HISTORY HAVE TO DO WITH VALENTINA ARDENNES, WHO IS, AS YOU SEE, A WOMAN WHO VERY MUCH LIVES IN THE PRESENT?
WHY, THAT'S B-BECAUSE...

MY EMPLOYER WANTS THAT PAINTING.
HE'S P-PREPARED TO OFFER A VERY HANDSOME SUM IF YOU USE YOUR CH-CHARMS TO FIND A WAY TO...

ELSEWHERE...
BOULANGERIE
Café
...STEAL IT?

HAVE YOU, INSPECTOR B.D. BELGIQUE OF THE SPECIAL POLICE--
--CALLED UPON THE NEFARIOUS THIEF BANDETTE TO STEAL A PAINTING?
CE N'EST PAS VRAI! CAN THIS BE TRUE?
I AM ASTONISHED! EVEN INCREDULOUS!

LOOK!
BANDETTE EATS THE CROISSANT OF DISBELIEF!

BUT I AM BEING CRUEL.
THIS MUST HAVE BEEN MOST DIFFICULT, COMING TO THE WORLD'S GREATEST THIEF FOR HELP, SO IT IS HELP YOU WILL HAVE.
AS FOR ME, I WILL HELP MYSELF TO YOUR CROISSANT, BECAUSE I ATE MY OWN TO MAKE A POINT.

OH. THERE IS JAM INSIDE!
MUNCH MUNCH MUNCH

NOW, TO OUR LARCENOUS BUSINESS. WHY DO YOU WANT THIS PAINTING? YOU MUST TELL ME.
IT WAS...IT WAS...

IT WAS HOW HIS GRANDFATHER PROPOSED TO HIS GRANDMOTHER!
HE PAINTED A VIGNETTE OF HIMSELF GIVING HER A RING! TOOK HER TO SEE THE PAINTING IN A GALLERY!
SO THRILLING! SO ROMANTIC!

"A COVERT MESSAGE OF LOVE GIVEN FROM A MAN TO A WOMAN. BUT DISPLAYED IN PUBLIC."
"A SECRET AND A STATEMENT, BOTH... CONTAINED IN A PAINTING!"

AH, THEN. THIS MATTER IS DECIDED. THE PAINTING WILL BE STOLEN.
WE SHOULD HAVE SEVERAL CROISSANTS TO CELEBRATE, NO?

ELSEWHERE...

AHH, THERE YOU ARE.

I BROUGHT THE MONEY. IT'S ALL HERE. AS WELL AS THE OTHER PAYMENTS YOU SUGGESTED.
WE WILL NEED TO HAVE THE PAINTING IN OUR POSSESSION WITHIN THE MONTH.
ANYONE WHO GETS IN YOUR WAY, WELL...YOU WILL KILL THEM, OF COURSE.

GOODBYE.

STEP
STEP
STEP-STEP
STEP

THE NEXT DAY...
YIP!
THUPP
THUPP
THUPP

AND SO...
AN INVITE, FOR ME?
YIP!

AND...
TOSS!
PUT PUT PUT PUT PUT
Party
OH! AN INVITE!

PLUS...
MATADORI
YOU ARE INVITED!
(IF YOU ARE NOT MATADORI, YOU WILL PLEASE IGNORE THIS POSTER—THOUGH PERHAPS ADMIRE MY DRAWING OF PIG.)

MOREOVER...
I HAVE CANDY BARS, CANDY BARS, AND CANDY BARS.
I BELIEVE THAT WILL DO FOR PARTY PREPARATIONS, YES?
YIP!

AND...
MATADORI
YOU ARE INVITED!
tap tap
tap

LATER...
KNOCK KNOCK CLANGG

?
!
VRRRRRRR...

?
!
VRRRRRRRKUNK

SO, LET ME GET THIS STRAIGHT...
YOU'RE LEAVING TO STEAL A PAINTING, BUT YOU WANTED TO HOLD A PARTY AS AN ALIBI?
I DON'T UNDERSTAND. YOU NEVER GET CAUGHT, SO YOU DON'T NEED AN ALIBI.
AND HOW IS A SECRET PARTY AN ALIBI?
AHH, YOU DO NOT UNDERSTAND? BUT IT IS SO SIMPLE!

THE PARTY HAS NOTHING TO DO WITH THE SIMPLE THEFT OF THE PAINTING...
BUT INSTEAD, SOMETHING FAR MORE SIMPLE.
ALIBI PARTY

THIS!
SMEKK!

YOU SEE? I HAVE GIVEN YOU A KISS.
THERE IS SCANDAL!
BUT MY ALIBI IS THAT THIS IS A PARTY, AND THAT KISSES AT PARTIES DO NOT COUNT. SO YOU SHOULD NOT BECOME OVERLY ENTHUSED.

LATER...

OH HO! AN OWL?
HAVE YOU COME TO SHARE YOUR WISDOM?
I WILL GO FIRST.

IF YOU DO NOTHING BUT FOLLOW THE RULES, YOU WILL ALWAYS BE BEHIND.

AND NOW, I AM AFRAID THAT I MUST DEPART.
THERE IS A SPECIAL POLICE INSPECTOR WHO IS WAITING FOR ME, AND I MUST NOT DISAPPOINT HIM.
ALWAYS BE TRUE TO YOUR FRIENDS.

THIS SECOND LESSON HAS BEEN GIVEN FOR FREE.

...SO I TOLD HIM THAT MAYBE WE SHOULDN'T GO DANCING ANYMORE, ON ACCOUNT OF HOW HE LOOKED LIKE A PANDA BEING ELECTROCUTED WHEN HE DANCES.
NO. ESTELLA. PLEASE TELL ME YOU DID NOT SAY THAT.

I DID. WAS THAT WRONG?
HE KNOWS I LIKE PANDAS SO I THINK IT WAS FINE TO SAY.
THIS IS TRAGIC. WE WILL BE DISCUSSING THIS FOR THE REST OF THE NIGHT.
YOU SHOULD TEXT HIM RIGHT NOW.

SHOULD I?
TELL HIM...
TELL HIM YOU HAVE A HORRIBLE INJURY THAT MAKES YOU SAY RIDICULOUS THINGS.
NAB!

EHH?

HEY!

HERE. I'LL TEXT HIM THAT YOU'LL COOK DINNER FOR HIM.
NO! I COOK LIKE... LIKE...

"...LIKE A PANDA BEING ELECTROCUTED."

HUPP!

TIP TIP TIP

OH?
THWOOSH!
THUMP!

!

OH, BUT THAT WAS CLOSE!

I ALMOST LOST A CANDY BAR!
SWIPE!

MUNCH
MUNCH
MUNCH

SHOOMP

I SHALL CALL DANIEL, AND INFORM HIM THAT MORE CELEBRATIONS ARE IN ORDER.
AND ALSO PERHAPS A THIRD ROUND OF CELEBRATIONS, TO CELEBRATE OUR SECOND CELEBRATIONS.
HOO HOO!
WHO? WHO?
BUT, I HAVE ALREADY ANSWERED!
IT IS DANIEL WHO I CALL.
HE HAS A MOTOR SCOOTER, AND IS PERHAPS NOT A FOOL.
HOO HOO!
I TELL YOU IT IS DANIEL THAT I CALL.
DO YOU NOT LISTEN?

HMM?

THE PAINTING?
WAVE
WAVE
WAVE

TAP
TAP
TAP

ONE BLOCK AWAY.
YOU DID WELL WITH THE DISTRACTION, NOODLES.
THE FEMME FELON THANKS YOU.

beep
beep
boop

BELDA, PIMENTO, HUSH. BANDETTE IS CALLING.
ring
ring
ring
SNORT
SNORT
SNORT!
BARK
BARK
BARK!
YIP
YIP
YIP!

HELLO? DANIEL! IT IS I! BANDETTE! THE WORLD'S MOST FLUMMOXED THIEF!
I REGRET TO REPORT THAT...

"...THE PAINTING HAS ESCAPED!"

THIS WOULD SEEM TO BE FAR ENOUGH.
CERTAINLY WE HAVE LOST ALL PURSUIT.
IT HELPS TO HAVE A PAIR OF EYES SUCH AS YOURS, DEAR NOODLES.
WE DON'T NEED THESE ANYMORE! HELP YOURSELF!
DON'T MIND IF I DO!
YOU!

IN THE NIGHT, YOU MISS NOTHING.

WALLENBEE. BRING THE CAR AROUND.
THE MISSION IS ACCOMPLISHED.
THE FEMME FELON HAS PROVEN HERSELF!

SOON, THE NAME OF THE FEMME FELON WILL BE RANKED AS THAT OF THE GREATEST OF THIEVES.
?
CREAK

HOO!
HOO!
YES, NOODLES! THAT IS THE QUESTION!
WHO IS THE FEMME FELON?
AND NOW, WITH THIS THEFT, MY LEGACY IS ASSURED AND THE TRUTH CAN BE TOLD!
WHY, I AM A SECRET IN THE NIGHT!

I AM A MYSTERY!
WE DON'T NEED THESE ANYMORE!

I AM AN UNPARALLELED THIEF!
!
CLICK
WE DON'T NEED THESE ANYMORE! HELP YOURSELF!
YOU!

MEANWHILE...
DANIEL! I HAVE COME TO BELIEVE THAT I, BANDETTE, HAVE BEEN THE VICTIM OF A CRIME!
THE PAINTING HAS BEEN STOLEN!
IT IS OUTRAGEOUS!
I FUME!

THIS IS MOST FUN!
SUCH AN UNEXPECTED TURN! HOW AMUSING!
WAIT, I THOUGHT YOU WERE MAD.

IT IS TRUE! THIS IS SO.
WELL, YOU CAN'T BE MAD AND HAPPY.
WHICH IS IT?

AHH, DANIEL, ARE YOU STILL AT THE PARTY?
YES.
THEN PLEASE IF YOU WILL, TAKE A LOOK AT THE ARTWORKS ON THE WALL.

OKAY. BUT, WHY?
PLEASE CHOOSE ONE, AND ONLY ONE.

HMM. ONLY ONE? BUT THEY'RE ALL SO NICE.

EXACTLY, DEAR DANIEL.
AND IT IS NOT THE WAY OF A WOMAN TO BE IN ONE SINGLE MOOD.

THERE ARE SO MANY! LIKE PAINTINGS ON WALLS!
WHY CHOOSE ONLY ONE?

MEANWHILE...
IT'S GONE!
GONE!

SCRREEEEECH!

WALLENBEE! IT'S GONE!
WHAT? WHAT'S GONE?

THE PAINTING!
IT'S BEEN STOLEN!
MY DEBUT IS RUINED!
ALL THESE YEARS OF TRAINING AND I GREW OVER-CONFIDENT!
WAVE
WAVE
WAVE

£#%ø*!!
THAKKK!

SLAMM!!

HOME.
TAKE ME HOME.

HERE IS YOUR DRINK, VALENTINA.
COMPLIMENTS OF THOSE MEN AT THE BAR.

"THEY BASICALLY FOUGHT OVER THE RIGHT TO BUY YOU A COCKTAIL."

HOW SILLY. MEN ARE SILLY.
REMIND ME TO SMILE AT THOSE SILLY MEN, LATER.
I WILL. NOW, ARE YOU GOING TO TELL ME WHY YOU KEEP LOOKING OUT THIS WINDOW?
NO. OF COURSE I WILL NOT.

"HAVEN'T I GIVEN YOU THE LESSON ABOUT MYSTERY? YOU SEE... A WOMAN NEVER TELLS."

NNNN.

STEP
STEP
STEP-STEP
STEP

STEP
STEP
STEP-STEP
STEP

STEP
STEP
STEP-STEP
STEP

STEP
STEP
STEP-STEP
STEP

STEP
STEP
STEP-STEP
STEP

STEP
STEP
STEP-STEP
STEP

tink
TO BE CONTINUED.

CHAPTER TWO

SKRASH!

THWAKK!

SKRASH!

HNNG?

NUDGE

TAP TAP TAP

HURRG?
FWANG!

PLUNGE

SPLOOSH!

STEP
STEP
STEP-STEP
STEP

HNGG.

STEP
STEP
STEP-STEP
STEP
STEP
STEP
STEP-STEP
STEP

STEP
STEP
STEP-STEP
STEP
SKRUTCH

HSS
CRKK
HSS

STEP STEP
STEP-STEP
STEP
BOOT!

HSSS
HSSS
CRKK
HSSSS
CRKK

STEP
STEP
STEP-STEP
STEP

STEP
STEP
STEP-STEP
STEP
THWAK!

HSSSS!!

HSSS!!

HSSS
HSSS
HSSSS
HSS
CRKK
HSS
CRKK
HSSS
HSSSS

CRKK
HSSSSSS
CRKK
CRKK
HSSS
CRKK
HSSS
HSSS

KRAKK!

STEP
STEP
STEP-STEP
STEP
THUNKK!

STEP
STEP
STEP-STEP
STEP
HNGG

MEANWHILE...
VOILA!
PREPARE TO BE AMAZED!
I HAVE PREPARED A MAGNIFICENT AND MOST ILLUMINATING LIST!

YOU SEE, MY DANIEL, THERE ARE ONLY SO MANY THIEVES WHO COULD--QUITE TEMPORARILY--STEAL FROM BANDETTE.
SCANDALOUS ROGUES, THEY ARE!
SCOUNDRELS!
INCORRIGIBLE MAKERS OF MISCHIEF.

ALSO QUITE TALENTED, AND WORTHY OF ALL DUE RESPECT.

AND NOW, AS YOU SEE, I HAVE MADE A LIST OF ALL POSSIBLE SUSPECTS.
THRUST!
I HAVE EVEN ADDED MY TALENTS AS AN ILLUSTRATOR TO CAPTURE THEIR LIKENESSES!

THIS IS A LIST OF YOUR FAVORITE CANDY BARS.

AHH, THIS IS TRUE.
I HAVE BEEN MUCH DISTRACTED.

Bandette's ME! Most Favorite Bars of Candy!
1. Chocobolik
Chocobolik
2. Caramel Avalanche
Caramel AVALANCHE!
3. Chocobolik Again!
Chocobolik
4. Empress of Blandings
Empress of Blandings
5. All Natural Bare Bars
6. Dean O's
DEAN O'S

MEANWHILE...
BAR • BRA
HA HA HA HA

VALENTINA, YOU'RE LEAVING? WITH THEM?
BUT...YOU SPENT THE WHOLE NIGHT JOKING WITH ME ABOUT WHAT LITTLE WORTHLESS BOYS THEY ARE!
IT'S TRUE, TILDA. I DID.

BETWEEN THE TWO OF US THEY ARE STILL NOT WORTH MY TIME.
THEY HAVE HORRIBLE JOKES...
...AND I COULD EASILY SUGGEST BETTER COLOGNES THAN THE HOG SPITTLE THOSE TWO ARE WEARING.
BUT...

...THEY DO HAVE WHAT I NEED.
wink

AHH! YOU MEAN...
I DO NOT MEAN WHAT YOU ARE TOO TIMID TO SAY.
NOT THAT, NO.
THAT I CAN FIND STREWN ABOUT THIS CITY LIKE PUDDLES AFTER A RAINSTORM.

NO, WHAT THESE BOYS HAVE IS A CAR...

BAR • BRA
...AND A WILLINGNESS TO LET ME DRIVE.

MEANWHILE...
£#%ø*!!

I CAN'T BELIEVE I CALLED THAT CRIMINAL BANDETTE TO STEAL A PAINTING!
ME! INSPECTOR B.D. BELGIQUE, CONSORTING WITH A KNOWN THIEF!
AN EXCEPTIONALLY TALENTED THIEF!

¡#β%ø*!!
THOKK!

THERE'S ONLY ONE THING THAT COULD POSSIBLY CALM ME NOW, AND RELIEVE THIS RAGE IN MY HEART.
YES?

AND OF COURSE YOU, LT. PRICE, KNOW WHAT I MEAN.
I...THINK I DO?

PUNCHING SOME CRIMINALS IN THEIR %ø#¡& FACES!
OH.
YES.
OF COURSE.

AND SO...!
OOP!
THOKK!

AND...
$&#π@!!
WE SURRENDER!
WE SURRENDER!

MEANWHILE...

CREAK

SCREEEEEEE...
UNFF!
FLIP!

WOOOO! WOO-WOO WOOOOO!
HA-HA-HA HA-HAH!
EERRRT!

!

I WILL BE UP IN A MINUTE, YOU TWO HANDSOME ROGUES. PREPARE SOME COCKTAILS, WILL YOU, AND...
I DO APOLOGIZE FOR MY POOR PARKING JOB. I'M JUST SO TIPSY!

BUT NOW I MUST PHONE MY ROOMMATE AND LET GENEVIEVE KNOW THAT I AM QUITE SAFE, PROTECTED BY TWO STRONG MEN, AND...
...THAT I SHALL NOT BE HOME FOR THE ENTIRE EVENING!

11
CLIKK

IT IS DONE.
I HAVE ACQUIRED THE PAINTING, WITH THE UNWITTING HELP OF TWO DECIDEDLY UNWITTING BOYS.
11

NO, THERE WAS NO TROUBLE AT ALL. IT IS TOO EASY TO TWIST A MAN, WITH THEIR DESIRES, THEIR HOPES.
IT TAKES NOTHING BUT A SINGLE SMILE, AND THEY BECOME MERE PUPPIES.

I DON'T EVEN NEED TO PET THEM! I JUST--
UMPFF!

!
NNNN.
THUD

MICHAEL THE BRUTE!
I'LL BE...NNN... TAKING THAT PAINTING.

OH NO YOU DON'T!

NNNN!
ZZZ-ZZZAKK

VALENTINA! WHAT'S HAPPENING? WHO'S THERE? VALENTINA!

THWAKK!!

DON'T...NNN... ANGER ME AGAIN, OR YOU'LL...NNN... FIND OUT WHY I'M CALLED THE BRUTE.

WAIT!

YOU'RE RIGHT, I WAS CRUEL.
I'M SORRY. IT'S JUST THAT I'M SO... IMPULSIVE.

SOMETIMES MY EMOTIONS GET THE BEST OF ME.
IT'S LIKE I CAN'T CONTROL MYSELF.

MAYBE YOU COULD...HELP ME?
WITH MY EMOTIONS. WITH MY... FEELINGS?
YOU'RE SO STRONG.
I'D BE SO GRATEFUL.

BUT I NEED TO KEEP THAT PAINTING, OR I'LL BE IN TROUBLE.
I DON'T WANT TO BE IN TROUBLE.
I WANT TO BE A GOOD GIRL.

I COULD TRADE YOU SOMETHING, IF YOU LIKE. I WANT TO BE FAIR.
I WANT TO SEE YOU SMILE.
I WANT YOU TO KNOW THAT I'M GOOD. TO REMEMBER ME.

I COULD TRADE YOU A KISS FOR THE PAINTING.
WOULD YOU LIKE THAT?
TO HOLD ME? TO PRESS YOUR LIPS TO MINE?
THEN YOU WOULD HAVE MY KISS, AND I WOULDN'T BE IN TROUBLE.
YOU WANT A KISS, DON'T YOU?
YOU DON'T WANT ME TO BE IN TROUBLE, DO YOU?

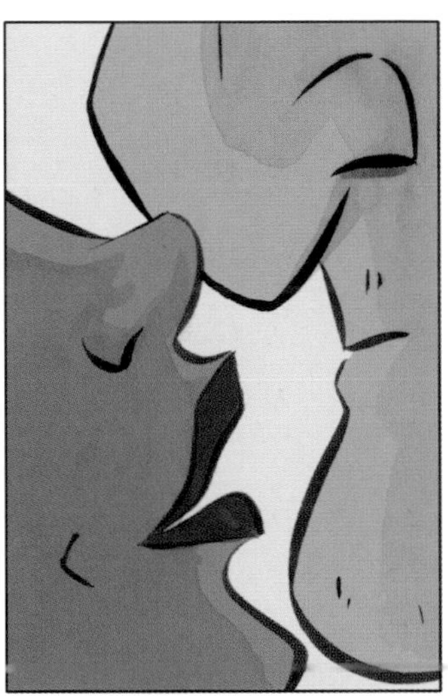

I DON'T CARE.

NOW STAY...NNN... OUT OF MY WAY, OR YOU GET THE BRUTE.
WHAT?
UNFF!

HE...DIDN'T CARE?

VALENTINA! ARE YOU THERE? WHAT JUST HAPPENED?

I...
I THINK I JUST FELL IN LOVE.

THE NEXT DAY...!
GONCOURT RESEARCH LIBRARY

PIMENTO, THERE IS MORE TO BEING A MASTER THIEF THAN SIMPLY STEALING. THERE IS RESEARCH TO BE DONE!
EXCUSE ME, YOU CAN'T BRING A DOG IN HERE.

THEN I WILL NOT!
PIMENTO ENTERS UNDER HIS OWN POWER!
THIS PROBLEM IS SOLVED.

SOON...
I HAVE ASSEMBLED SKETCHES AND PHOTOS OF THE PAINTING THROUGH THE YEARS.
AND I HAVE ASSEMBLED EYEWITNESS TESTIMONIALS OF THE MEANINGS OF SEVERAL CHANGES THE PAINTING HAS ENDURED.
AND I HAVE ASSEMBLED SEVEN PASTRIES FROM THE COMMISSARY, OF WHICH I WILL ONLY ALLOW MYSELF THE BEST SIX, FOR I AM KNOWN AS THE SAINT OF RESTRAINT.

AND SO...
MUNCH MUNCH MUNCH

PLUS ALSO...
MUNCH MUNCH MUNCH

FURTHERMORE...
MUNCH MUNCH MUNCH

AND THEN...
PIMENTO. THERE HAS BEEN A GREAT SUCCESS!
AFTER SEVERAL HOURS OF STUDYING THE WEALTH OF MATERIAL...

...I HAVE EATEN ALL SEVEN OF THE PASTRIES.
YIP!

NOW, I MUST MAKE A SELECTION OF *TRÈS IMPORTANT* PHONE CALLS, BUT FIRST I MUST **CHANGE**.
YOU WILL PLEASE CAUSE A **DISTRACTION**.
YIP!

?
YIP!
YIP!
YIP!
RUSH
RUSH
SPIN
RUSH

YIP!
YIP!
YIP!
?
RUSH
RUSH
SPIN
RUSH

!
YIP!
YIP!
YIP!
RUSH
RUSH
SPIN
RUSH

AND SO...
AH, *OUI*! *BONJOUR* AND **SALUTATIONS**! THIS IS *BANDETTE*! THE MASTER **THIEF**!
I HAVE NOW BEEN **STUDYING** FOR SOME TIME, AND A **MOST SIGNIFICANT FACT** HAS **OCCURRED** TO ME!
!
YIP!
YIP!
YIP!
RUSH
RUSH
SPIN
RUSH

I WISH TO PLACE AN ORDER FOR **SEVEN** *ÉCLAIRS*, **TWELVE MACAROONS, ONE ENTIRE PAN** OF *MILLE-FEUILLE*, **TWO** LEMON TARTS, AND A **SIZEABLE BAG** OF ASSORTED **CHOCOLATES**.
I BELIEVE THAT WILL **DO**. UNLESS YOU THINK I SHOULD ADD **MORE**, IN WHICH CASE I WOULD HONOR YOUR **JUDGMENT** IN THIS MATTER.

BEEP
BOOP

HELLO, MY **URCHINS**! IT IS *I*, THE **UNPARALLELED THIEF**! THERE IS **MUCH** TO **DISCUSS**!

IT'S *BANDETTE*!

OH! *BANDETTE*!

I'M LISTENING!

AND ALSO...
ring
ring
ring

BELGIQUE, HERE.
IT IS BANDETTE! I HAVE BEEN DOING RESEARCH AND EATING PASTRIES!
ONLY ONE OF THESE IS PERTINENT TO OUR CONVERSATION BUT STILL I FEEL THAT BOTH ARE WORTHY OF MENTION.
BUT NOW, INSPECTOR, YOU WILL PLEASE OPEN YOUR WINDOW.

MY WINDOW? WHAT FOR?
PLEASE, INSPECTOR, THIS IS MOST IMPORTANT.
NOW THEN. I HAVE LEARNED, THROUGH STUDY OF THE ARTIST'S STUDIO PAINTING, THAT IT HOLDS A MATTER OF GREAT IMPORT IN THE WORLD TODAY.

IT DOES?
YES! IT IS TRUE!
FOR THE SCOUNDREL WHO HAD THE PAINTING ON DISPLAY HAS A POLITICIAN IN HIS POCKET.
A MEMBER OF THE SENATE!
IT IS SCANDALOUS.
OUR NATION WILL SHUDDER WHEN THIS NEWS IS RELEASED!

"THE GANGSTER AND THE POLITICIAN HAVE BEEN USING THE PAINTING TO SEND MESSAGES, YOU SEE, MESSAGES OF NATIONAL SECRECY, IN RETURN FOR LARGE SUMS OF MONEY AND THE ATTENTIONS OF CERTAIN WOMEN."

£#%ø*!!
VIBRANTLY SAID, INSPECTOR BELGIQUE!
IT IS NOW EVEN MORE IMPERATIVE THAT I RECOVER THE PAINTING, SO IT MAY BE USED IN EVIDENCE TO END THIS CORRUPTION.
ALSO I SHOULD MENTION AGAIN THAT THE PASTRIES WERE DELICIOUS, AND THAT THERE ARE MORE ON THE WAY.

HMMM.

WHERE ARE YOU?
I THOUGHT YOU WANTED ME TO OPEN THE WINDOW SO YOU COULD COME INSIDE?
NON! THIS IS NOT NECESSARY.
I HAVE BEEN BEHIND YOU THIS WHOLE TIME!

I ONLY CONSIDERED YOU SHOULD HAVE SOME FRESH AIR, FOR IT IS HEALTHY!
AND I HAVE BEEN DISCARDING YOUR CRAYMORE CIGARETTES, FOR THEY ARE NOT.
&#%#$@!

HOURS LATER...

MUNCH
MUNCH
MUNCH

I AM LEAVING YOU THREE PASTRIES.
YOU MUST DECIDE HOW TO SPLIT THEM YOURSELVES.
IT IS MY HOPE THIS WILL NOT CAUSE A RIFT IN YOUR RELATIONSHIP.

AU REVOIR.

BONSOIR!
PANTAGRUEL'S TAROT READS
YOUR DESTINY DECODED!

WAVE
WAVE
WAVE

BANDETTE.
MICHAEL!
MANY GREETINGS!
YOU HAVE SOMETHING I WISH TO STEAL.

DON'T YOU, NNN, KNOW I'M A BRUTE?
I WON'T, NNNN, LET YOU.
I KNOW NO SUCH THING.
IT IS PERHAPS THE CASE THAT YOU ARE STRONG, BUT ALAS FOR YOU, I AM A TRUE THIEF.
AND THAT, NNNN, MEANS?

I WATCH.
I SEE.

YOU PRETEND TO BE THE BRUTE, BUT THAT IS MERELY A TRICK. A DECEPTION. A DEVICE YOU USE TO STEAL.
TO, NNNN, STEAL?

YES. IT'S TRUE WHAT I SAY.
YOU USE YOUR SUPPOSED BRUTISHNESS AS A VEIL.
OTHERS UNDERESTIMATE YOUR INTELLIGENCE, AND THEN... VOILA!
THE BRUTE PLUCKS THE COIN OF CAUTION FROM THEIR POCKETS!

BUT I NOTE THE GRACE OF YOUR WALK.
THE SPARK IN YOUR EYES.
THE TIMING OF YOUR SUPPOSEDLY UNEDUCATED GRUNTS.
EVEN YOUR SCENT.

MY, NNN, SCENT?
IT IS THAT OF COAL. AND TOBACCO. AND GASOLINE.
BUT YOU WEAR IT AS A MASK. A FAÇADE! MY NOSE IS AS NIMBLE AS MY FINGERS, AND MY NOSE DETECTS...
...THE UNMISTAKABLE AROMA OF CRÈME BRIOCHE CAKES FROM CAFÉ CORTO ON THE RUE RASPUTIN.

I SUBMIT THAT NO BRUTE WOULD SIT AT SUCH A FINE CAFÉ!
NOR WOULD A BRUTE BROWSE THE SHELVES OF THE VOTRE PETIT RÊVE BOOKSTORE, WITH ITS DISTINCTIVE ATMOSPHERE OF DECAYING PAPER AND AGARWOOD INCENSE...
...WHICH I RECALL FROM THE TIME I WAS LIBERATING A SMALL ASSORTMENT OF HANDWRITTEN JULES VERNE LETTERS.

YOU'RE SMARTER THAN I WOULD HAVE THOUGHT.
THAT IS FREQUENTLY THE CASE WHEN IT COMES TO BANDETTE.
I AM OFTEN MUCH SMARTER THAN EVEN I THINK MYSELF!

STILL, INTELLIGENCE IS NOT ALWAYS WHAT WINS THE DAY.
EVEN IF YOU MATCH ME IN TERMS OF BRILLIANCE, EVEN IF YOU'RE MY EQUAL IN THE ARTS OF DECEPTION, I'M STILL BY FAR YOUR SUPERIOR IN TERMS OF PHYSICAL STRENGTH...
...AND YOU'LL HAVE TO FIGHT ME FOR--

YOUR PARDON.
I WAS NOT LISTENING.
I WAS INSTEAD INSPECTING THIS PAINTING.
WHA? HOW?

AHH. YOU MEAN...HOW HAS IT COME INTO MY POSSESSION? BUT THIS WAS EASY.
YOU WERE SPEAKING WHILE I WAS STEALING.
A SIMPLE MATTER OF PRIORITIES.

GIVE THAT BACK!
OF COURSE!
BUT I WILL ONLY STEAL IT AGAIN. IT IS MY WAY.
YOU PRACTICE THE ARTS OF BEING A THIEF, BUT IT IS SIMPLY WHO I AM.

WHAT YOU ARE IS A FOOLISH YOUNG GIRL.
ONE I ADMIT I ADMIRE, BUT...

YOU MAY HAVE CAUGHT THAT I ONLY PLAY THE FOOL, BUT AN ACTOR STUDIES HIS ROLE, SO I KNOW WHAT A FOOL LOOKS LIKE...
...AND I CAN SAY WITHOUT DOUBT THAT YOU HAVE DONE A VERY FOOLISH THING.
OH?

YOU SPEAK OF THE CHOCOLATES, YES? I HAVE EATEN SEVEN, AND THAT IS FAR TOO FEW.
I ADMIT MY IMPRUDENCE IN THIS MATTER.

NO, BANDETTE. IT'S NOT THAT.
IT'S THAT YOU'VE ALLOWED YOURSELF TO BE STEERED INTO DANGER.

SO CAUGHT UP IN CONVERSATION YOU DIDN'T NOTICE WHERE I WAS WALKING US, WHERE I WAS GUIDING US.

ALONE. IN THIS ALLEY.
AGAINST A MAN WHO WILL KEEP THIS PAINTING, AND KEEP HIS SECRETS.

I HAVE GIVEN THIS MATTER SOME THOUGHT.
IT IS QUITE CLEAR TO ME NOW.
I SHOULD HAVE HAD TEN CHOCOLATES.
I WILL ADJUST MY BEHAVIOR IN THE FUTURE.

JOKE IF YOU WANT, BANDETTE.
BUT AS TO YOU HAVING A FUTURE,WE'LL SEE ABOUT--

CLICK!

NNN?

CLICK!

OH?

CLICK!
CLICK!
CLICK!

THIS IS INSPECTOR GAINES OF THE GRAND POLICE MINISTRY!
YOU WILL LIE DOWN ON THE GROUND, FACE FIRST!

YOU ARE SUSPECTED OF HAVING MATERIAL SENSITIVE TO THE SECRETS OF THIS NATION!
PREPARE TO BE TAKEN INTO CUSTODY! SURRENDER YOURSELVES!
ON THE GROUND, NOW, OR WE WILL OPEN FIRE!
POLICE
POLICE
POLICE
POLICE
POLICE

"THERE WILL BE NO FURTHER WARNINGS!"
TO BE CONTINUED!

CHAPTER THREE

BANDETTE, GET *DOWN!*

"THE **GRAND POLICE MINISTRY**... *NNN*...ARE *SERIOUS!* THEY WILL **OPEN FIRE** IF...*NNN*...YOU DON'T *SURRENDER!*"

FACE **FIRST!**
ON THE **GROUND!**
NO SUDDEN **MOVES!**
HANDS UP! GIVE YOURSELF UP **NOW!**
YOU WILL BE **SHOT** IF YOU DO NOT **SURRENDER!**

WAVE
WAVE
WAVE

WHAT ARE YOU DOING?

I HAVE A **QUESTION.**
A...WHAT? BE *SERIOUS,* YOUNG LADY! THIS IS **NATIONAL SECURITY** AT STAKE!
ON THE GROUND, *NOW!* OR WE **OPEN FIRE!**

WAVE
WAVE
WAVE

SIGH.
WHAT'S YOUR QUESTION?

BALLOONS.
BALLOONS?
THAT'S NOT A **QUESTION.**

HUH? BALLOONS?
YOU SEE!? IT IS A QUESTION!

POP!

POP! POP!
POW!
BANG POP! BANG
BANG BANG BANG
POW!

PING! POP!
RUN!
ZING!

PIP!
YES, OF COURSE WE RUN, NO?
THE CORPORATIONS ARE THEIVES!
POP!
BUT, SUCH AGITATIONS! THIS WORD IS MISSPELLED!

PAP! POW! POP!
BANG! BAT-TA-TAT
POP!

IT IS JUST THAT I AM VERY PARTICULAR ABOUT THIS WORD!
SSSSSSSSS
THIEVES
SPAKK
CRAKK
POP!

BANG!
POP!
PAP!
ZING
NNN!
ZIP
WHUMP!
POL

BANDETTE!
WE ARE HERE!
DID YOU LIKE THE BALLOONS?
BANG!
ZING!
OUI! SUCH A FESTIVAL!
POP!

CRAK!
POP!
YIP!
YIP!
YIP!
OH?
POP!
BANG
POP!
WAG
WAG
WAG
PING!

DON'T MOVE!
NO.
I CANNOT AGREE.
POP
POP
EXERCISE HAS MANY BENEFITS.

PAP!
POP!
CRAK!
BANG
THUMP!
POW
POP!
OOF!

POP!
AHH, BUT NOW YOU HAVE CEASED MOVING, DESPITE MY EARLIER ADVICE.
POP!
OOOOOO...

WITNESS MY ESCAPE!
SCAMPER!
POLICE
LICE

OH?

YOU ARE NOT WITNESSING!
THIS IS A REMARKABLE FAILURE ON YOUR PART!

SOON...
Kuijpers' Café
NOK NOK NOK

IT'S BANDETTE! @*&%#!
I CAN'T BE SEEN WITH HER!
GO OUTSIDE AND SEE WHAT SHE WANTS BEFORE SHE DRAWS ATTENTION TO--

INSPECTOR BELGIQUE!
IT IS I, THE GREAT THIEF BANDETTE!
I HAVE RECENTLY ESCAPED THE GRAND POLICE MINISTRY IN ORDER TO BRING YOU THIS PAINTING YOU HIRED ME TO STEAL!
¡π@£#!!

THUMP

$ß#£*&!!!

AH, SUCH LANGUAGE, INSPECTOR!
TAKE CARE! THERE ARE THOSE WHO MAY OVERHEAR YOU!

BUT TO THE MATTER AT HAND. I HAVE DELIVERED THE PAINTING AND YOU ARE NOW IN MY DEBT.
A THIEF OF MY STATURE COMMANDS ASTRONOMICAL SUMS.
I SHALL BE SATISFIED BY NOTHING LESS THAN...

...THIS CHOCOLATE AND BANANA MUFFIN.
OH?
WELL, I SUPPOSE THAT'S FINE. IF THAT'S ALL YOU--

PLUS YOU MUST STOP SMOKING.

AND SO, SOON...

HER *PRICE* WAS FAIR.
SHE RISKED HER *LIFE*.

£#$*@!! I'LL THROW *HALF* THE PACK AWAY. ONE MUST **EASE INTO** THESE THINGS.
HALF THE PACK? THAT WILL NOT **DO**.
BANDETTE HAS INSTRUCTED ME TO CALL YOUR *MOTHER* UNLESS YOU COMPLY WITH HER **RULES**.

WHAT? #$%^@! BANDETTE IS NOT YOUR **COMMANDING OFFICER!** THAT WOULD BE *ME*.
AND IF YOU CALL MY **MOTHER**, THEN AS YOUR **SUPERIOR** I WILL--

BEEP
BEEP
B-DOOP
BEEP

Σ#$*@!!
FINE! IT'S **DONE**!
HANG UP THE **PHONE**!
HELLO? BONJOUR? WHO IS CALLING?
TOSS!

HEH.
MY MOTHER.
THE DRAGON.
IT WILL BE NICE TO SEE HER SMILE AGAIN.
BECAUSE YOU'VE QUIT SMOKING?

THAT'S STILL TO BE DETERMINED.
BUT, NO...I MEANT SHE'LL SMILE ONCE SHE HAS THAT PAINTING HANGING ON HER WALL AGAIN.
THIS PAINTING?

YES.
IT'S TRUE THAT I HAD BANDETTE STEAL IT, BUT IN GREATER TRUTH IT LEGALLY BELONGS TO MY FAMILY.
OR AT LEAST, IT SHOULD.

"A MAN NAMED RASTON STOLE IT. HE PRESENTED PAPERS SAYING THAT HE HAD PURCHASED IT DURING THE WAR."
"IT WAS PURE $#&@£! HIS PAPERS WERE FORGED."
"BUT HIS FORGED PAPERS WERE BETTER THAN OUR FAMILY'S PAPERS, WHICH DID NOT EXIST AT ALL."

"...AT LEAST IN THE EYES OF THE JUDGE WHO PRESIDED OVER THE TRIAL. IT WAS PLAIN THERE WAS A KICKBACK INVOLVED."
BANG
BANG
BANG

"IT BROKE MY MOTHER'S HEART."
"THAT BLANK SPACE ON HER WALL."

BUT IF THE PAINTING IS YOURS, THEN--
WAIT!
THOSE FOOTSTEPS?
STEP
STEP
STEP-STEP
STEP

GUHH!
WHUMP!

UNFF!
THUMP!

IL TREDICI!

RUN, HELOISE!

KICK!
UNGG!!!

GRAB!

CLAMP!

URKK!
SQUEEZE!

GAHH!
THUMP!!
!?

HNGG.

HELOISE! RUN!
HE'S A KILLER!

I'M TAKING YOU DOWN!
WHUMPH!

HUH?
OH ¡$@&#!!

GRAB!

NO!
SMACK!

CLAMP!

IL TREDICI!!
URGK
SQUEEZE

URK

HNGG.

YOU'RE GAMBLING THAT I'M TOO MEEK TO PULL THIS TRIGGER AND TAKE A HUMAN LIFE?
PERHAPS THAT IS TRUE.

BUT I AM NOT TOO MEEK TO TAKE YOUR LIFE IF IT SAVES THAT OF BORIS DUCHAMP BELGIQUE.

DROP

STEP STEP
STEP-STEP
STEP
PANT
PANT
WHEEZE

ELSEWHERE...
??

!!!

AHH? YOU CHOOSE THE WHITE?
NON, THIS CANNOT BE TRUE! PERHAPS IT WILL MATCH THE MEAL, BUT RED IS THE COLOR OF PASSION!
DO YOU WISH PASSION, OR A CULINARY MEDAL? THIS IS A DECISION YOU MUST MAKE.
??

AND YOU MUST MAKE IT ALONE, FOR BANDETTE'S PHONE NOW RINGS.
ringg
ringg
ringg

HELLO? YES? HELOISE?
BUT WHAT IS THIS? IL TREDICI? THE STRANGLER?
THIS IS AN OUTRAGE!

I FUME!

ELSEWHERE, IN THE BLISTERED BARNACLE BAR...

IS *THIS* SEAT TAKEN?
HNGG?
TAP TAP TAP TAP

I'LL TAKE YOUR GRUNT AS CONSENT.
VALENTINA? WHAT ARE YOU... *NNN*...DOING?

PROPOSING AN *ALLIANCE*.
I'VE JUST RECEIVED WORD THAT *IL TREDICI* NOW HAS THE PAINTING.
WE WILL *BOTH* LOSE THE SIX FINGER SECRET IF WE DON'T...

...*COMBINE* OUR EFFORTS.
NNNG.

WELL SAID. PROBABLY.
BUT, LISTEN, YOU INTERESTING MAN. BETWEEN US WE ENCOMPASS BOTH SEX AND STRENGTH.
CERTAINLY BETWEEN THE TWO OF US, WE CAN FIND IL TREDICI'S WEAKNESS.

YOU ACT LIKE A LITTLE GIRL, THINKING... *NNN*...THAT ALL PROBLEMS HAVE SOLUTIONS.
THE STRANGLER ...NNN...*HAS* NO WEAKNESSES.

"NOT SEX."

"NOT ANY LACK OF STRENGTH."

"NOT FOOD OR DRINK OR DRUGS."

"HE HAS NO VICES."
"NO GREED."
"NO DESIRES."

"HE LIVES, BREATHES, AND WALKS... ONLY TO DESTROY."

HMM. THERE MUST BE SOMETHING.
DO YOU WANT TO GO SOMEWHERE AND...DISCUSS THINGS?

THIS DISCUSSION IS OVER.
OOO!

STRUCK OUT, HUH?
STRUCK GOLD, MORE LIKE IT.
SIGH.

STRUCK GOLD, MORE LIKE IT.
SIGH.

HMM.

HMM, INDEED!
AHH!

WHAT ARE YOU DOING HERE?
HOW DID YOU EVEN KNOW WHERE I WAS?
TEST QUESTIONS?
BUT THE ANSWERS ARE SO SIMPLE!

YOU HAVE BUGGED VALENTINA, BUT I HAVE BUGGED YOU, AND I HAVE BEEN LISTENING TO A BUG OF THE BUG!
AHH, SO MANY BUGS!

SHALL WE CROUCH HERE LONGER, THEN? IS THIS HOW YOU SPEND YOUR TIME?
IT'S BETTER THAN SPENDING MY LIFE BY RECKLESSLY JUMPING INTO DANGER.
IN THIS I AGREE WITH MICHAEL, THE BRUTE.
IL TREDICI HAS NO WEAKNESS.

AH, YOU PLAY THE *HUMBUG?* I AM SADDENED.
DO YOU NOT **UNDERSTAND,** MY DEAR MONSIEUR, THE **SOLUTION?**
AFTER **ALL,** YOU LISTENED TO THE SAME CONVERSATION. OUR EARS WERE **PRACTICALLY TOUCHING!**
THE KEY IS THAT IT'S *TRUE,* WHAT THAT **FAUX BRUTE** HAS SAID.

"IL TREDICI IS A MAN WHO EXISTS **ONLY** TO *DESTROY."*

AND **THEREFORE** HE NEEDS SOMETHING *TO* DESTROY.

"OR HE WILL *NOT* EXIST."

POOF!
GONE.

BANDETTE *DEPARTS!*
BUT I HAVE LEFT A **CANDY BAR** TAPED TO YOUR **HEAD,** SHOULD YOU BUILD UP AN APPETITE DURING YOUR ADMIRABLE **CROUCHING!**

EH?

HOO HOO!
WHO? IT IS I, BANDETTE!
AND HELLO AGAIN TO YOU, DEAR OWL.
YOUR COMPANY IS ALWAYS WELCOME.

WILL YOU COME ALONG WITH ME?
I HAVE SEVERAL MISSIONS OF MOST DIRE IMPORTANCE.

MY FRIEND DANIEL IS FOND OF CHOCOLATE COVERED CARAMEL, SO I MUST HAVE FOUR OF THOSE...
...AND SIX OF THOSE.
...WHILE I AM PARTIAL TO CHOCOLATE COVERED CHOCOLATES, SO I REQUEST THREE OF THOSE, OR PERHAPS TEN MORE THAN THREE.

AND NOW, AN IMPERATIVE THEFT!

TILLIEUX ZOO
ENTRÉE

THERE. I HAVE STOLEN FIVE MINUTES OF A BABY HIPPO'S TIME.
THERE ARE FEW GREATER TREASURES.

BUT NOW AT THIS MOMENT, STAY AS SILENT AS YOUR CUSHIONED FEATHERS ALLOW!
FOR BANDETTE MUST STEAL THIS NATION'S GREATEST MASTERPIECE!

THERE! A CANDY RECIPE FOR WHICH I HAVE DEVELOPED AN INTEREST!

BUT NOW, THE MAIN EVENT.
IF YOU PAY CLOSE ATTENTION, I WILL TEACH YOU THE TRUE SPIRIT OF A MASTER THIEF.

HELLO. MY NAME IS BANDETTE.
EH? A GIRL?

I HAVE OBSERVED YOU FROM THAT TOWER THIS PAST WEEK.
IT IS MY BELIEF THAT YOU HAVE FALLEN OFF A BIKE.
EH? A *BIKE?*

TRUE. YES. THIS IS SO.
HOW LONG SINCE YOU HAVE STOLEN A KISS?
EH? A *KISS?*

AND SO IT IS DECIDED. YOU HAVE FALLEN OFF THE BIKE OF STOLEN KISSES, AND MUST GET BACK ON.
STEALING IS AN ART, AFTER ALL, AND ART TAKES PRACTICE.
YOU HAVE LOST YOUR MOMENTUM. YOU NEED TRAINING WHEELS.
I SHALL PROVIDE THEM.

YOU MAY STEAL A KISS.

SMEK

THERE! YOU ARE ON YOUR BIKE AGAIN. BUT YOU *MUST* MAINTAIN PRACTICE!
PERHAPS YOUR NEXT TARGET COULD BE THE WOMAN IN THE WHITE SHAWL, WHO I HAVE ALSO WITNESSED SITTING ALONE?

EH?
HMM. MAYBE SO.

THERE. I HAVE SPOKEN OF BICYCLES, MADEMOISELLE FRANCHESTER.
THANK YOU, BANDETTE.

AND THEN, SOON...

HOOO HOOO

HOO?

OH?
RATS?

SHIF
SQUEE

I'M NOT SURE I UNDERSTAND WHAT--
BUT, OH? DO YOU WANT ME TO FOLLOW? YES?
SO BE IT. I AM YOURS TO COMMAND.

SQUEE
SQUEE
SQUEE

SQUEE
SQUEE
SQUEE
SQUEE

OH?

HNGG.

SQUEE
SCRITCH
YOU DON'T LIKE HIM?
IT IS TRUE THAT HE IS A *SCOUNDREL.*

STILL, A *FORMIDABLE* OPPONENT. ONE MUST TAKE CARE.
IT WOULD BE *FOLLY* TO FACE OFF AGAINST SUCH A STRANGLER **ALL ALONE.**

MUNCH
MUNCH
MUNCH

STEP

?
THWUMPHH!

FOLLY IT IS.
TO BE CONTINUED!

PIGALLE
L'AMOUR
ET
L'AMITIÉ

chapter four

I SUPPOSE WE FIGHT NOW?
IS THIS YOUR WISH?

WE HAVE SEVERAL ALTERNATIVES.
YOU COULD RELINQUISH THIS PAINTING, FOR INSTANCE.
OR PERHAPS WE COULD HOLD A CONTEST FOR POSSESSION, YES?
TAP TAP
DO YOU SING OPERA? PLAY MARBLES? BAKE PASTRIES?

OR... NO! I HAVE IT!
WE SHALL HAVE A DRAWING CONTEST!

I AM WELL KNOWN FOR MY TALENTS AT ILLUSTRATING PIGS.
THIS VICTORY IS UNMISTAKABLY MINE.
DO YOU SUBMIT?

THWOOSH
AH. YOU SWAT INSTEAD?
PERHAPS YOU ARE A CRITIC?

WHAT'S THIS? AGAIN?
THWOOSH
CHKK CHKK

YOUR PARDON, IL TREDICI. THERE SEEMS TO BE SOME MISTAKE.
I AM NOT SOME BOTHERSOME FLY TO SWAT.
DODGE
THWOOSH
I AM INSTEAD A CHARMING THIEF AND PROFESSIONAL PIG ILLUSTRATOR.

I AGAIN REFER YOU TO THE DRAWING I HAVE JUST NOW COMPLETED, ADDING A COMPONENT OF MUD, OF WHICH PIGS ARE FOND.

YANK!
OH?

HMM?
GRAB!

WHAMM!!
OH, DISASTER!
THIS CANNOT BE!

YOU WERE EATING A SPICY BURRITO?
THIS IS NOT HEALTHY, IL TREDICI.
YOU SHOULD BE ASHAMED.

I POKE YOU WITH A FORK.

HNGG!?
CHKK
CHKK
CHKK

AND NOW, PERHAPS YOU WILL BE AMAZED BY MY SCAMPERING POWERS?

FOR, LIKE THE MOTHER KILLDEER, I LEAD THE PREDATOR AWAY...
SCAMPER SCAMPER DANCE
STEP STEP STEP-STEP STEP

"...FROM THE VULNERABLE."

YIP!

TUG TUG TUG TUG

TUG
TUG

TUG TUG TUG

ROLL
ROLL
ROLL
ROLL
YIP!
YIP!
YIP!

LEAP!

ROLL
ROLL
ROLL
ROLL

CLIMB
CLIMB
CLIMB
ROLL
ROLL
ROLL
ROLL

CLOSE BY...
QUIT...NNN... FOLLOWING ME, VALENTINA.

I'M NOT FOLLOWING YOU, MICHAEL. WE'RE WALKING SIDE BY SIDE, BUT YOU HAVE LONGER LEGS.
THAT'S...NNN... NONSENSE.

AND NO MORE OF YOUR ...NNN...FLUTTERING EYES OR DEEP BREATHS.
I AM A BRUTE, NOT A FOOL.
YOU WILL NOT CONVINCE ME TO...NNN...CHALLENGE IL TREDICI FOR THAT PAINTING.

IT IS TIME YOU...NNN... REALIZE THE GAME IS LOST. WE HAVE FAILED.
THE PAINTING IS NOW...

...OUT OF OUR REACH?
ROLL ROLL ROLL ROLL

GRAB IT!
YIP?

WHAT LUCK! WE HAVE THE PAINTING!
IT'S LIKE A BLESSING FROM LAVERNA, THE GODDESS OF THIEVES!
YIP! BARK! YIP!

A BLESSING TO ME, YOU MEAN!
BECAUSE ALL LAVERNA HAS DONE FOR YOU...

...IS TAKE YOU FOR A RIDE.
EEP!
KICK!
?

HNNH.
BEEP BOOP BEEP

HELLO. THIS IS MICHAEL.
YES. THE BRUTE.
I HAVE ...NNN... NEWS.

I HAVE THE PAINTING.
IN MY POSSESSION.
AS I SPEAK.

I FORESEE NO FURTHER...NNN... PROBLEMS.

BLOCKS AWAY...
GASP! SHOTS RING OUT!
A MISS!
A DODGE!
A CLOSE CALL!
A CHOCOLATE CANDY BAR WITH CARAMEL FILLING!

YOU CONTINUE TO MISS, IL TREDICI.
I AM FORCED TO BELIEVE THAT YOUR HEART IS NOT IN THIS GAME.
BANG
CRAKK
BANG

YOUR LOVE IS IN STRANGLING, BUT MY NECK IS NOT WITHIN REACH.

HNGG.

BANG!

SNAP!!

OH, HOW UNFORTUNATE!
A PROBLEM SOLVER!

HOW CURIOUS TO BE FALLING.

THIS, OF COURSE, IS AN EMERGENCY.
CLIKK!

ELSEWHERE...
QUIT BALLET, MANON? THIS CANNOT BE!
I LOVE THE BALLET, ADALIND. I DO.
BUT THE MOVES ARE SO PRECISE. RIGID!
I LONG FOR MORE EXPRESSION. SOME MADNESS.

MADNESS IS LEAVING BEHIND THE BALLET!
OH! MR. WAITER WITH THE STRONG CHIN, PLEASE TELL THIS WOMAN SHE IS CRAZED.
NOT GOING TO DO THAT.

OH. YES. I SUPPOSE YOU CAN'T.
IT MIGHT AFFECT YOUR TIP IF YOU INSULT A CUSTOMER BY CALLING HER CRAZY.
IT'S NOT AN INSULT TO BE CRAZY!
I TELL YOU, THAT'S MY POINT! I WANT MADNESS IN MY DANCE! I WANT CHAOS! I WANT...

...BANDETTE?
THE EMERGENCY SIGNAL!

SHE IS... FALLING?

ELSEWHERE...
FALLING?

HOW CAN THIS BE?
PEANUTS!
WAAAAH!
Choco Nuts

LISTEN, MY URCHINS. THE SITUATION IS DIRE, AND I HAVE LITTLE TIME.
YOU MUST DO AS I ASK!

MANON! ADALIND! KIYOMI!
THERE IS A CREPE SELLER'S CART ON THE CORNER NEAR THE MARY CASSATT EXHIBITION! A POLICEMAN STANDS NEARBY!
PLEASE DISTRACT THIS MAN!

FRECKLES! DALTON!
ACQUIRE BIRDSEED BY ANY MEANS REQUIRED, EVEN BY LEGAL MEANS, IF NECESSARY!
AND THEN YOU MUST FEED THE PIGEONS, FOR THEY ARE MUCH DISTRESSED BY NOISY GUNFIRE AND PLUMMETING THIEVES.

OH!
CROISSANTS!

MY DANIEL! YOUR JOB IS MOST IMPORTANT!
I'M LISTENING, BANDETTE!
ZOOM!!

YOU WILL PLEASE PROCEED AT ALL GOOD SPEED TO THE REAR DOOR OF FEYNMAN'S FINE ANTIQUITIES!
RAD THAI
WHOOSH!

WHERE A WOMAN IN BLACK WILL GIVE YOU AN ENVELOPE.
DO NOT OPEN THIS ENVELOPE UNDER ANY CIRCUMSTANCES, AND AWAIT FURTHER INSTRUCTIONS.

HELLO, PIGEON.
YOU LOOK WELL TODAY.
BUT AHH, THERE IS SOMETHING BANDETTE IS FORGETTING!

OH! YES!
FALLING!

BUT NO MORE!
RIP!!
GRAB!
Works of Power
A MARY CASSAT EXHIBIT
GRAVITY, I MOST RESPECTFULLY DECLINE YOUR INVITATION.

BONSOIR, TOURISTS!
WAVE WAVE
PLEASE TO DUCK YOUR HEADS!
WHOOSH!
CLIK! CLIK! CLIK!

AH, FLIGHT!

?
OH HO! WE MEET AGAIN!

THOOP!

BOOP!
MWRR!
Cat's Crepes

YOUR PARDON! I HAVE INTRUDED. MOST RUDE!

LEAP!
I SHALL PREPARE AN APOLOGY.
?

Cat's Crepes

I PRESENT YOU WITH A PAINTING BY MARY CASSATT IN APOLOGY FOR THE USE OF YOUR UMBRELLA.
I AM FORGIVEN NOW, NO?

MEANWHILE...

MICHAEL THE BRUTE!
STAY RIGHT WHERE YOU $#&@£π ARE!
NNNN!
SPECIAL INSPECTOR B.D. BELGIQUE?

YOU ARE COVERED FROM THREE #&@*% WINDOWS, YOU $#*@&!
MAKE THAT FOUR #&@*% WINDOWS, NOW!

DOWN ON YOUR KNEES!
GET YOUR #&@*% HANDS BEHIND YOUR HEAD!
NNNN...

SNEAK
SNEAK
SNEAK
LIFT!

NO MOVING!
DON'T SO MUCH AS BLINK, YOU Σ%$*&!

HOO! HOO!
WHO, YOU ASK, NOODLES?
IT IS I, THE ILLUSTRIOUS FEMME FELON!
YOU DID WELL TO FOLLOW THE PAINTING!

WALLENBEE! IT WORKED PERFECTLY! THE RECORDING FOOLED HIM!
I AM A MASTER THIEF!

YOU SHOULD HAVE SEEN ME!
THE BRUTE IS A MONSTER, BUT I HAD NO FEAR!

I WAS SOMEWHAT WORRIED HE WOULD TURN AROUND, I'LL ADMIT.
AND WHAT IF THE RECORDER HAD SKIPPED, OR RUN OUT OF POWER?
OR IF SOME ONLOOKER CALLED OUT, "BEWARE, BRUTE, SHE IS FOOLING YOU!"

SO I SUPPOSE I HAD SOME FEAR, BUT THEN AGAIN OVERCOMING FEAR IS WHAT BEING A MASTER THIEF IF ALL ABOUT!
I, THE FEMME FELON, HAVE STOLEN FEAR ITSELF!
NO, THAT DOESN'T MAKE SENSE.
YOUR PARDON, WALLENBEE. I FIND MYSELF OVERLY EXCITED.

BUT THE IMPORTANT THING IS, IF THIEVES HAD ANNALS OR YEARBOOKS, I WOULD NOW BE CONSIDERED A MASTER CLASSMAN!
WISE FEMME FELON! FEARLESS FEMME FELON! THE KEENEST OF THIEVES, WITH HER ALL-SEEING OWL, AND HER DAUNTLESS BUTLER WALLENBEE!
START THE CAR! WE WILL ABSCOND WITH THE LOOT, AND DRIVE OFF INTO HISTORY!

HMM? MY KEYS?
HOO!
PAT
PAT

WAVE
WAVE
HONK
HONK

RRRROOAARR!!

OH DARN IT.

SHIFT!

!
MUNCH
MUNCH

?
SHAKE
SHAKE
POINT!

I WILL NOT ALLOW THE PAINTING TO BE STOLEN FROM ME, BANDETTE.
ALL THIS CHATTER!
CAN WE NOT SIMPLY ENJOY THE DRIVE?

I STOLE A CANDY BAR FROM INSIDE YOUR CAPE.

I HAVE STOLEN YOUR SHOES.
WHAT?
HOW?!

THIS PAINTING, THIS ONE HERE IN YOUR CAR, I FIND IT AMUSING.
PAINTINGS ARE A WAY OF EVOKING FEELINGS IN OTHERS.
THE FLUSH OF KNOWLEDGE. OF EMPATHY.
A HUMAN CONNECTION.
EACH STROKE OF THE BRUSH IS A MESSAGE, FROM THE INNER CHAOS OF VAN GOGH TO THE COMPASSION OF LUCIAN FREUD.

AND YET, THIS PAINTING, THE SIX FINGER SECRET, HAS EVEN MORE DEPTH.
IT IS MORE THAN A MESSAGE. IT IS A MESSAGE BOARD.
WHIRLS OF MEANING PUT INTO PLACE. ERASED. REPLACED. IT IS A DOCUMENT.
LIKE EVERY SINGLE BITE OF A CHOCOLATE BAR BRINGING THE TASTE OF A NEW HIDDEN FRUIT.

DO YOU KNOW, MONSIEUR, THERE'S A MARRIAGE PROPOSAL ON THAT CANVAS, PAINTED BY BELGIQUE'S GRANDFATHER TO HIS GRANDMOTHER?
ASTOUNDING.

THERE IS ALSO A MESSAGE THAT COULD TOPPLE A CURRENT KINGDOM, WERE THE MESSAGE KNOWN TO THE PUBLIC.
A MATTER OF IMPROPRIETY WITH FUNDS.
NOT ALL THIEVES, IT MUST BE SAID, ARE CHARMING.

SPEAKING OF THIEVES, SIX OF US NOW CONTEST FOR THIS PAINTING.
THERE IS MYSELF, AND OF COURSE YOU, MONSIEUR, WITH YOUR IMMENSE TALENTS AND BARE FEET.

"AND THERE IS MICHAEL, KNOWN AS THE BRUTE, THOUGH IN TRUTH HE IS BUT A FACSIMILE OF BRUTISHNESS."
"HIS TRUE NATURE IS AS DEEP AS THE SWIRLS OF COLOR ON A VAN GOGH PAINTING."

"AND VALENTINA ARDENNES-- WHAT A WOMAN!"
"SHE USES HER SENSUALITY AS A CLUB."
"MOST MEN AND NOT A FEW WOMEN HAVE PROVEN EAGER TO BE BRUISED."

"IL TREDICI, OF COURSE, CAN BARELY BE CONSIDERED A THIEF."
"MORE A LOOTER, PERHAPS? A ROBBER. A PLUNDERER."
"THAT MAN IS ALMOST ARTFUL IN HIS ARTLESSNESS."

"THE FEMME FELON I ADORE. I FEEL WE COULD BE FRIENDS. SISTERS.
"SHE'S A FLEDGING THIEF, BUT ALL CHILDREN TODDLE ABOUT AT FIRST, AND IT IS ALWAYS MOST AMUSING TO WATCH. SHE IS THE CAT VIDEO OF THIEVES."

NOW, MONSIEUR, BOTH MY CANDY BAR AND MY TALK HAVE FINISHED.

AU REVOIR!

EEEEEERRTT!!

SCRITCH
SCRATCH

MEANWHILE...
MADAME DE POMPADOUR
EXHIBIT

GUARD THIS ALCOVE, PIMENTO, IF YOU WOULD PLEASE.

GRRRR...

AH, HERE IT IS!
MADAME DE POMPADOUR, 1721-1764
Multi-lensed, multi-colored opera glasses.
Purpose unknown.

ALL PURPOSES ARE UNKNOWN, DON'T YOU THINK?
LIFE IS SUCH A MYSTERY. IT IS ALSO A CELEBRATION.
YIP!

"A CELEBRATION DESERVING, I BELIEVE, OF FIREWORKS."
FWOOSH!!
EH?

HURGH?
SPAK!
SPAK!
SPAK!
SPAK!

STAMP!
STAMP!
STAMP!
STAMP!

WHAT WAS THAT?
NOT SURE. SOME KID'S PRANK, LIKELY.
BE ALERT, THOUGH.
IT MIGHT HAVE BEEN A DISTRACTION.

AU REVOIR, MR. MUSCULAR SECURITY GUARD. I HAVE ENJOYED YOUR EXHIBIT.
HAVE A GOOD DAY, YOUNG LADY.

DID YOU HEAR? SHE CALLED ME MUSCULAR.
HAH! YOU? IF SHE THINKS YOU'RE MUSCULAR, THEN...

"...SHE NEEDS EVEN THICKER GLASSES."

HUH?

BANDETTE'S **EMERGENCY WATCH**? HOW DID *THIS* GET ON MY WRIST?
SHE MUST HAVE PUT IT THERE EARLIER?

I'LL SAY **ONE THING**, SHE *DOES* HAVE TALENT.
ALTHOUGH SHE'S ALSO **INFURIATING**. AND **RECKLESS**.
THAT GIRL HAS A *TOTAL* DISREGARD FOR *PROPRIETY*.

I SUPPOSE I'VE SAID MORE THAN ONE THING.
BUT I MUST ADMIT, IN ALL HONESTY, **BANDETTE** IS--

HUH?!

ERRRRTTT!!

ARE YOU *ALL RIGHT*?
I DIDN'T *SEE* YOU!
YOU JUST CAME OUT OF **NOWHERE** AND--

HNGG.

IL TREDICI!

THAKK!
HAHH!

HNGG.

!!
GRAB!

SLAMM!!
UGH!
KRRNNCH!!

PUNCH
PUNCH
PUNCH

HEHH.

GRAB!

CLIKK
TO BE CONCLUDED!

CHAPTER FIVE

EXCUSE ME, PIGEONS!
I AM ZOOMING!
RAD THAI
ZOOOM!

I SHALL NEED NOT ONLY HASTE, BUT SUPPLIES AS WELL.
VRRRRNN

HMM. ADORABLE BABY PIG TRADING CARDS.
THIS SKETCH BY VERMEER.
MY FATHER'S GRADUATION RING.
SEVERAL CANDY BARS.
SOME EMERALDS I'D FORGOTTEN.
BUT, OH! HERE WE ARE!
WOOSHHH!

THIS BIRDSEED I BORROWED FROM FRECKLES AND DALTON. AND...
RAD THAI
VVRRRN...

...THIS HONEY, WHICH I ACQUIRED EARLIER FROM A CREPE CART, IN CASE I ENCOUNTERED SOME WARM BISCUITS.
HONEY

VOOOMM!

SQUIRT!

NGHH?
THE HONEY!
SKIIIIIID!
TURN!

TOSS!
NGHH?
THE SEEDS!
WOOOSH!

NGH?

HNGHH.
DRIP
DRIP

BUZZ
FLAP
FLAP
FLAP
NGH!
SWARM
FLAP
PECK
BUZZ
PECK
PECK
SWARM
FLAP
BUZZ
PECK
COUGH COUGH!
FLAP
BUZZ
FLAP
FLAP
SWARM
BUZZ
FLAP

HELLO! I DID NOT BELIEVE YOU WOULD WISH TO BE STRANGLED, SO I HAVE ARRIVED FOR A DRAMATIC RESCUE!

NOW, MONSIEUR, WE LEAVE IL TREDICI TO HIS LESSONS OF THE BIRDS AND THE BEES, AND...
ZOOOM!
...ESCAPE!

I GRABBED THE PAINTING! AND, WE'RE SAFE NOW, SO...
SLOW DOWN!
SLOW DOWN? BUT I AM NOT SPEEDING!
I KNOW THIS BECAUSE I AM NOT LICENSED TO DRIVE.
YOU CANNOT SPEED IF YOU ARE NOT DRIVING!
WOOSH!
ZOOOOM!

MY LOGIC IN THIS MATTER IS FLAWLESS.

"I MIGHT ADD THAT YOU WERE QUITE FORTUNATE, MONSIEUR, THAT I WAS WITH DANIEL WHEN HE RECEIVED THE DISTRESS CALL.
"HIS MOTOR-SCOOTER HAS A GPS ATTUNED TO THE EMERGENCY WATCH, SO I WAS ABLE TO LOCATE YOU BEFORE IL TREDICI DID TOO MUCH DAMAGE."
BZZZ BZZZ

LET THIS BE A LESSON THAT STEALING IS WRONG.
SWIPE!
WOOSH!
SKID!
ZOOOM!

GIVE THAT PAINTING BACK!
AND SIT DOWN!
SIT DOWN? BUT WHY?
AS I EARLIER EXPLAINED...

...I AM NOT DRIVING.
LEAP!
!!
RAD THAI
ZOOOOM!

MUNCH MUNCH
GAHH!
WOOSH!
SKID!
ROAR!

TWO HOURS LATER...

THE FEMME FELON
(AND NOODLES)

VALENTINA ARDENNES

MICHAEL
THE BRUTE
GENTS

WE KNOW WHY WE'RE HERE. WE'VE EACH BEEN DEFEATED.
SOUNDLY THRASHED, REALLY.

ONE MIGHT EVEN SAY, REBUFFED.
NNN.

THE SIX FINGER SECRET, HIDDEN IN THAT PAINTING BY PIERRE SUBLEYRAS, HAS BEEN BOUNCING BACK AND FORTH BETWEEN US ALL.
IT'S RIDICULOUS. A FARCE.

LIKE ROMANCE.
NNN.

AND WHILE WE'VE ALL PROVED TO BE EACH OTHER'S FOIL, IT IS BANDETTE WHO IS OUR PRIMARY THREAT.
THAT GIRL IS UNCANNY.
IT IS CRUCIAL THAT WE REMOVE HER FROM THE GAME, SO THAT WE CAN MORE EASILY PLAY.

THOSE OF US WHO WANT TO PLAY, ANYWISE.
NNNN.
SLURP SLURP

TO THOSE ENDS, I HAVE PLANNED AN ATTACK THAT WILL STRIKE AT BANDETTE'S WEAKEST LINK.
HER ACHILLES HEEL, IF YOU WILL.

CHOCOLATE?
IMPRESSIONIST PAINTINGS?
PASTRIES?
THE JEWELS OF FAMOUS COURTESANS?
WHOO! WHOO!
flap flap

YOUR OWL IS CORRECT.
IT IS NOT WHAT THAT WE SPEAK OF, BUT...WHO?
AND THE ANSWER IS... HER FRIENDS.

AND WHILE IT IS IMPORTANT TO CONSIDER... OTHERS...
NNNN.
SLURP SLURP

"...IN THIS CASE WE CAN USE BANDETTE'S CONCERN FOR HER FRIENDS AGAINST HER."
"EARLIER TODAY, I PLACED A LISTENING DEVICE, DISGUISED AS A BARRETTE, IN THE HAIR OF ONE OF BANDETTE'S FRIENDS."
AH. YOU LIKE KITTIES, DO YOU?
HERE CHILD, A GIFT FOR YOU.

PRETTY!

"NOW, WE NEED ONLY LISTEN, AND BANDETTE'S SECRETS WILL BE LAID BARE."

Le Macaron Sensual
CLOSED for Private Party!

¡#ß%ø*!! CLOSED FOR SOME Σø#¡& PARTY?!
ISN'T THIS THE RIGHT ADDRESS?
Macaron Sen
IT IS. AND THIS IS WHERE SHE SAID TO MEET, SO I THINK WE'RE INVITED TO THE PARTY?

HELLO?

AH, YES! DEAR HELOISE! EQUALLY DEAR AND SOMEWHAT GRUFF SPECIAL INSPECTOR BELGIQUE!
COME IN! ENTREZ S'IL VOUS PLAIT! EVERYONE IS HERE!

"MY DANIEL! FRECKLES, WHO OWNS THIS BOULANGERIE! MATADORI, WHO IS NOT A CRIMINAL, AND SHOULD NOT BE ARRESTED! THE THREE BALLERINAS! BELDA! DALTON! SIMONE!"

PIMENTO! PIETRO! THESE THREE CATS I FOUND LURKING! TWO PIGEONS WHO WERE INVITED BY MISTAKE!
THIS RODIN STATUE I FOUND ON THE WAY HERE!

"THESE PASTRIES! THIS PYRAMID OF CANDY BARS!"
"A CHOCOLATE RABBIT, WHICH IS PUZZLING THE MISTAKENLY INVITED PIGEONS!"

AND THIS PAINTING BY PIERRE SUBLEYRAS, TITLED THE ARTIST'S STUDIO, BUT KNOWN TO A SELECT FEW AS...
THE SIX FINGER SECRET!
YOU HAVE IT AGAIN!

FREEZE!
NOBODY MOVE!
IN THE NAME OF THE GRAND POLICE MINISTRY, I ORDER YOU...

AHH, INSPECTOR GAINES!

HERE IS SOME PIE.

I TRUST YOU WILL NOT MIND IF I PLACE THIS PIGEON UPON YOUR HEAD?
SHE HAS BEEN RECKLESSLY PECKING AT THE CANDY BARS. YOU WILL ARREST HER IF SHE CONTINUES.

NOW THEN! AS WE ARE ALL PROPERLY GATHERED, I WILL TELL YOU THE SECRET OF THIS CLEVER PAINTING!

IF YOU WOULD BUT PLEASE DIRECT YOUR ATTENTIONS TO THIS FIGURE HERE, UPON THE PAINTING.

YOU WILL SEE THAT HE HAS SIX FINGERS. EACH OF A DIFFERENT COLOR.

AND NOW WE WILL NEED MADAME DE POMPADOUR'S GLASSES, WHICH I REMOVED FROM A MUSEUM.
HEY! YOU STOLE THOSE!
OUI! BUT OF COURSE I DID. I AM BANDETTE!
NOW PLEASE, IT IS RUDE TO INTERRUPT, AND YOU WILL DISTURB YOUR PIGEON.

NOW THEN, MADAME DE POMPADOUR'S FASHIONABLE GLASSES, WHICH I'M QUITE CERTAIN SHE WOULD HAVE WANTED ME TO HAVE...
...COME EQUIPPED WITH MULTIPLE LENSES CODED TO CERTAIN COLORS.

MEANING THE GLASSES CAN DETECT CHANGES IN THE PAINT BY ADJUSTING TO EACH NEW LEVEL.
turn turn turn

"THUS, LAYERS OF CHANGES CAN BE REVEALED, OLDER MESSAGES ONCE THOUGHT LOST, NOW REVEALED BY PROPER CHROMATIC FILTERING! MOST INGENIOUS!"
My apartments after sunset

AND IF I MAY BUT PUT THESE SPECTACLES UPON YOUR EQUALLY INGENIOUS HEAD, INSPECTOR GAINES, I WILL SHOW YOU SOMETHING QUITE FASCINATING.
PLEASE REMAIN STILL DURING THIS PROCESS SO THAT WE WILL NOT AWAKEN THE PIGEON WHO ROOSTS IN YOUR HAIR.

THERE! DO YOU SEE?
UH OH.
OH NO.
THIS IS... MY GOD...THE SCANDAL!

IT IS SCANDAL!
PIETRO HAS EATEN ALL THE CAKE!

HE IS A PIG, BANDETTE.
OUI. TOO TRUE, MATADORI!
YOU ARE FORGIVEN, PIETRO.
OINK!

BUT THERE IS A MAN WHO CANNOT BE FORGIVEN. HIS NAME AND DEEDS ARE REVEALED IN THE PAINTING...
...WHICH IS NOW BEING GAZED UPON BY INSPECTOR GAINES OF THE GRAND POLICE MINISTRY, AND CLARICE THE PIGEON OF NO PARTICULAR ADDRESS.

"IT IS A SORDID TALE OF GRAND PARTIES, OF WHICH I AM FOND, BUT IN THIS CASE FINANCED WITH FUNDS STOLEN FROM THE PUBLIC, WHICH IS UNACCEPTABLY IMPOLITE."

"IT IS A TALE OF BRIBERY. OF MISAPPROPRIATIONS! AND ASSASSINATIONS! THE VERY REPUBLIC SHUDDERS!"

BUT, THERE IS ALSO GOOD NEWS!
I HAVE MANAGED TO PROVE, DEAR INSPECTOR BELGIQUE, THAT THIS PAINTING BELONGS TO YOUR FAMILY!
OH, LOVELY! HOW?

SIMPLY BY SIFTING THROUGH THE BELGIQUE FAMILY RECORDS--WHICH I PURLOINED--AND FINDING PHOTOS FROM THE PAST THAT FEATURE THE PAINTING IN THE BACKGROUND.
HERE! I WILL PROJECT SEVERAL SUCH SCENES ONTO A SCREEN, SO THAT WE MAY ALL REJOICE IN MY FINDINGS.
MAMA'S Records + Papers

THERE! YOU SEE!
THE PAINTING, SITUATED JUST BEHIND THE BEHIND OF A YOUNG BELGIQUE!

"AND HERE AGAIN! THE PAINTING! SEEN JUST BEYOND AN INFANT PERFECTING THE SQUALLS FOR WHICH HE WOULD LATER COME TO BE KNOWN!"
$ø#¡&!! BANDETTE!!!
NO NEED TO THANK ME!
WE ARE FRIENDS, AND DO WHAT WE CAN.

WELL, I'LL BE OFF. I NEED TO MAKE...A LOT OF CALLS.
HAVE FUN, BRAVE GAINES!
YOU MAY RETURN THE PIGEON AT ANY TIME.

CAN YOU TELL US WHO THIS GOVERNMENT SCOUNDREL IS?
BUT OF COURSE. I HAVE ALL OF THE IMAGES ON MY PHONE!
WITNESS!

NO. THOSE ARE PHOTOS OF CANDY BARS.
flip
flip
flip

HMM, PIGS, THIS TIME.
flip
flip
flip

OH, ONE OF MY DANIEL. I AM MOST EMBARRASSED.

PERHAPS ANOTHER TIME, THEN.
BORIS DUCHAMP BELGIQUE, I PRESENT THIS PAINTING TO YOU.
IT IS POLICE EVIDENCE, BUT YOU HAVE A BADGE, THEREBY THIS PROBLEM IS SOLVED.

BUT... NO.
YOINK!

PERHAPS IT IS BEST IF I AND MY URCHINS PROTECT IT FOR A TIME, AS THE OTHER THIEVES HAVE NOT YET BEEN DISCOURAGED, AND...

...I WOULD NOT WANT THEM TO INTERFERE.

LET ME TELL YOU EXACTLY WHERE WE WILL HIDE IT AWAY FROM THE CLUTCHES OF THE FEMME FELON, VALENTINA ARDENNES, AND MICHAEL, THE BRUTE.

THE NEXT DAY...
YOU STILL INSIST YOU WILL LEAVE THE BALLET, MANON?
OUI. I DO. I YEARN FOR MORE EXPRESSION.
BALLET WILL ALWAYS BE MY HOME, BUT I LONG TO TRAVEL!
THE PAINTING!

OH. I LIKE THAT. AND, I THINK I UNDERSTAND.
NO! THE MADNESS IS SPREADING!

EXCUSE ME, ANYONE? I MUST HAVE DIRECTIONS!
KIYOMI, WHAT ARE YOU DOING?
WAVE WAVE

I MUST ASK SOMEONE FOR DIRECTIONS TO SANITY, ADALIND, FOR IT IS CERTAIN THAT WE'VE PLUNGED INTO THE WOODS OF MADNESS, AND--

BUMP!

OOH.

MICHAEL THE BRUTE!
HE'S AFTER THE PAINTING!
RUN!

FIVE MINUTES LATER...
VALENTINA!
BUT, HOW? THE BALLERINAS JUST GAVE US THE PAINTING!

TEN MINUTES LATER...
HOW DO THEY KEEP FINDING US?!
THE FEMME FELON!
WAHH!!

HERE!
TOSS!

GET READY BELOW!
HURRY! DROP IT!

CATCH!
TOSS!

WE NEED BANDETTE!
WHY ISN'T SHE ANSWERING HER EMERGENCY SIGNAL?
WHERE IS SHE?

MEANWHILE...
HAVE YOU FIGURED OUT THE CODE?
NO. THIS LETTER YOU HAD ME PICK UP FROM WOMAN IN BLACK, IT'S...
...IT'S JUST A LIST OF CANDY BARS AND FAMOUS CIRCUS PERFORMERS.

AH, BUT CANDY BARS ARE MUCH MORE THAN ONLY A TREAT, AND WOMEN WHO RIDE TIGERS ARE MORE THAN SIMPLY ENTERTAINERS.
YOU MUST LOOK DEEPER, MY DANIEL, TO THE TASTE OF THE CHOCOLATE, AND TO THE TASTE OF THOSE TO WHOM DANGER IS THE SWEETEST KISS.

IF YOU WANT THE TRUTH OF THIS WORLD, YOU MUST DELVE INTO...

"...WHAT IS TRULY IMPORTANT."
BUZZZZZ!!
BUZZZZZ!!

BUZZZZZ!!
BUZZZZZ!!
EMERGENCY!

AND, SOON...
WE HAVE THEM.

YOU'RE TRAPPED.
GIVE US THE PAINTING, OR WE...

...WILL RELEASE THE BRUTE.
WE WILL?

WHY... WHY ARE THEY SMILING?
I DON'T KNOW. I MEAN, UNLESS...

OH CRAP.

HELLO!
HELLO, BANDETTE.

A TRAP, THEN?
A TRAP INDEED.

MY URCHINS AND I WERE PLAYING A GAME ALL ALONG!
AN EXTENDED PLOY TO LURE THE THREE OF YOU HERE TOGETHER.

AS WE KNEW YOU HAD PLANTED A LISTENING DEVICE.
PRETTY!

IN ORDER THAT YOU WOULD THINK MY URCHINS UNPROTECTED, I HAVE BEEN FLIRTING WITH DANIEL...
...GIVING HIM ADDITIONAL CLUES TO SOLVE A PUZZLE I'D PRESENTED HIM WITH.

I HAVE ALSO BEEN ILLUSTRATING OSTRICHES, FOR I FIND THEM TO BE CURIOUS AND AMUSING CREATURES.
THOSE NECKS! THEIR FASHIONS!

YOU MAY EACH HAVE A DRAWING.

AND NOW...
CLICK!

THANKS FOR THE PRETTY KITTY!

NOW THEN, IT IS PERHAPS TRUE THAT YOU THINK I AM YOUR GREATEST THREAT.
AFTER ALL, IT IS INCONCEIVABLE THAT YOU DO NOT THINK I AM THE GREATEST THIEF.
HOWEVER...

"...IT IS IL TREDICI WHO IS A FAR GREATER MENACE. HE STEALS YOUR VERY AIR."

"YOUR VERY LIFE."
13

IN SOMEWHAT RECKLESS FASHION, I'VE ALERTED THE STRANGLER TO OUR CURRENT LOCATION.
I NOW PAY YOU EACH THE SUM OF ONE CHOCOLATE BAR, IN COMPENSATION FOR THE NEED TO DEFEND YOUR LIVES.

THIS PAYMENT IS IN ADDITION TO THE OSTRICH DRAWINGS.

OF COURSE, YOU COULD SIMPLY RUN, BUT IL TREDICI WILL FIND YOU, IN THE END.
IT IS FAR BETTER TO FACE YOUR FEARS IN LIFE, SUCH AS STRANGLERS, OR IN PIMENTO'S CASE, LEMONS, WHICH FOR SOME REASON FRIGHTEN HIM.
YIP!

BESIDES, IF WE STAY TOGETHER, WE FIGHT TOGETHER.
WE MUST BE THICK AS THIEVES, OR AS THICK AS ONE OF THOSE DELICIOUS BELGIAN PASTRIES.

I BELIEVE YOU KNOW THE ONE.
NO.
SORRY.
NNN. YES.

NOW THEN, IN ORDER TO PASS TIME UNTIL THE MAN WHO WANTS TO MURDER US ARRIVES, I PROPOSE A TUTORIAL ON THE ILLUSTRATION OF OSTRICHES.

FIRST, YOU DRAW A CIRCLE. THEN GIVE IT FEATHERS. THE FEATURES SHOULD BE ASKEW, AS OSTRICHES ARE NOT BASTIONS OF GROOMING.

ADD TWO LEGS. NO MORE. NO LESS. THEY ARE QUITE SKINNY, LIKE TOOTHPICKS, STRAWS, OR THE JAPANESE TREATS KNOWN AS POCKY.

NEXT, A DECISION MUST BE MADE. WILL YOU BE GIVING YOUR OSTRICH A HAT? GLASSES?

WHERE ARE YOU GOING, FEMME FELON?
DO YOU FEEL THAT YOUR OSTRICH-DRAWING SKILLS HAVE REACHED THE MASTER LEVEL?

I'M SORRY, BANDETTE, BUT... SINCE THIS QUEST BEGAN, I'VE BEEN NOTHING BUT A FAILURE.
I LOOK AT YOU ALL, AND... YOU'RE SO GOOD! I...I REALLY DON'T BELONG WITH ANY OF YOU.
BAH! THIS IS NOT TRUE! I SPIT!

NO. I DO NOT SPIT, BECAUSE IT IS RUDE.
BUT THE POINT, FEMME FELON, IS THAT YOU ARE ONE OF US. TRULY AND FOREVER.

A THIEF IS A THIEF, AND A THIEF IS WHO YOU ARE.
A THIEF, OF COURSE, MAY STEAL ANYTHING SHE WANTS.
BUT ONE THING SHE SHOULD NEVER STEAL...

...IS HER OWN CONFIDENCE.

STEP
STEP
STEP-STEP
STEP

OH?

STEP STEP
STEP-STEP
STEP

PREPARE YOURSELF.

STEP
STEP
STEP-STEP
STEP
"IL TREDICI IS HERE."

PUNCH!
NGH!

HNNG.
!

SWOOP!
URK!
OOF!
GRAB!

SLASH!!
HRRR!

HANDS OFF MY MAN!

CRACK!

AHH! SERIOUSLY?!
MICHAEL! SAVE ME!

FEND FOR YOURSELF!
I DON'T ...COUGH COUGH... CARE ABOUT YOU!

YOU... YOU DON'T CARE?

AH! WHY ARE YOU SO PERFECT?!

GUHK!
GRAB!

HELLO! I SEE THAT IT IS TIME FOR ANOTHER INSTRUCTIONAL CLASS.
THIS TIME, I WILL TEACH YOU THE PROPER METHODS OF FIGHTING A SUPERIOR FORCE!
THE ANSWER IS...YOU DON'T.

YOU SIMPLY BRING BUTTER.
toss!
SPLATT!

SLURKK!
WHOOP!

AND A DOG...
YIP! GRR!
FLIP!
THUMP!

BITE!
HRRR!

AND A FRIEND...

...WITH A POINTY STICK.

PLEASE DO NOT MOVE, IL TREDICI.
AS YOU ARE A STRANGLER, I BELIEVE YOU WELL KNOW...

...HOW FRAGILE A NECK CAN BE.
TAP.

ARREST THAT MAN!
hustle hustle
STOMP

AND ONCE WE HAVE HIM SECURED, ARREST THOSE THREE AS WELL! THEY'RE ALL WANTED THIEVES!
OH.
HMM.
NNN.

CLICK!

OH! DID YOU CHECK FOR WEAPONS? EVERYONE ATTEND! YOUR ATTENTION ON ME, PLEASE!
IL TREDICI IS TRÈS DANGEREUX! CHECK FOR PISTOLS! KNIVES! CAKE FORKS! CAKE!

I SUPPOSE I SHOULD THANK YOU FOR LETTING ME KNOW THAT IL TREDICI WAS HERE.
AND I SUPPOSE I SHOULD APOLOGIZE IN ADVANCE FOR ARRESTING YOUR...

...FRIENDS?
¡$@&#!! WHERE DID THEY GO?
WHO KNOWS? CERTAINLY NOT I, BANDETTE, THE GREATEST OF ALL THIEVES AND THE VERY PICTURE OF INNOCENCE.

I HAVE DRAWN YOU AN OSTRICH.

LATER...

MADAME ROCHLAW. I HAVE YET TO RECOVER THE PAINTING.
MY REGRETS FOR THE DELAY, BUT--

OH. LT. PRICE?
UH, MADAME ROCHLAW?
CUFF!

A FOREIGN SPY, MONSIEUR.
INTENT ON ACQUIRING THE SIX FINGER SECRET AS A WEAPON OF BLACKMAIL.
SWIFF!

OH, AND SPEAKING OF BELGIQUE'S PAINTING, BANDETTE TELLS ME YOU'VE OFFERED TO CLEAN AND RESTORE IT, AS A GIFT TO THE INSPECTOR?
DID SHE SPEAK THE TRUTH?
ME? CLEAN AND RESTORE IT?
I...OH. AH. YES. BANDETTE IS RIGHT.

AS ALWAYS.

SIGH.

CREAAAK

AH, DANIEL. YOU SOLVED THE PUZZLE, THEN?
PARTIALLY? I MEAN, IT'S OBVIOUS THIS IS THE RIGHT ADDRESS, BUT...

...I THINK THERE WAS SOMETHING ABOUT...A LIST OF THINGS TO BRING?
I COULDN'T FIGURE THAT PART OUT. IT SEEMS TO BE...NOTHING.

BUT OF COURSE! THIS IS TRUE! MY DANIEL, WHAT COULD YOU BRING?
CHOCOLATES? PASTRIES?
JEWELS ONCE WORN AROUND THE NECKS OF CELEBRATED BURLESQUE PERFORMERS, OR ON THE HANDS OF FAMOUS COURTESANS? ALL FINE THINGS.
BUT I AM A THIEF, AND SUCH ITEMS ARE ALWAYS AND EASILY WITHIN MY GRASP.

NO. I WANT NOTHING MORE THAN TO SIT AND WATCH THE CITY TOGETHER, AND TO FEEL THE THRUM AND THE STOMP OF ROMANCE.

THE ONLY THING I WANTED IN YOUR HAND...

...IS MINE.

TWO WEEKS LATER...

THERE, MOTHER!
MONSIEUR AND BANDETTE WORKED TOGETHER TO REPAIR ALL DAMAGES, AND THE PAINTING IS ONCE AGAIN WHERE IT BELONGS.

OH, I'M SO PROUD OF MY BIG GROWN-UP BOY!
MY LITTLE GRUMPY-KINS! MY LITTLE--
Pinch Pinch
EH? BUT WHAT'S THIS?

THERE'S A PICTURE OF...YOU?
PINCH PINCH
HUH? OW! OW!

THERE! YOU! AS A THIEF! STEALING A HEART!

¡%@*Σ$!! I CAN'T BELIEVE IT! YOU BRING THE PAINTING BACK TO ME LIKE THIS?!
OUTRAGEOUS! ¡$@&#!! TO THINK I WAS PRAISING YOU!

¡$@&#!! WHERE'S MY WHISKEY CORDIAL? I FEEL FAINT! THIS IS ALL YOUR FAULT!
MY FAULT?! %@*Σ$! DO YOU KNOW HOW MUCH I WENT THROUGH TO GET THIS PAINTING?
$@&#! I NEED A CIGARETTE!
BUT WAIT, I CAN'T EVEN SMOKE ANYMORE BECAUSE I MADE A DEAL WITH A THIEF WHO RETRIEVED THIS PAINTING FOR YOU! ¡%@*Σ$!!

AND WHAT DO I KNOW ABOUT THAT PICTURE OF ME? BANDETTE MUST HAVE PUT IT IN!
ME? A THIEF? ABSURD! ¡$@&#!! AND WHOSE HEART WOULD I STEAL ANYWAY?

STAY TUNED FOR THE NEXT BANDETTE STORYLINE:
The Wedding of B.D. Belgique

URCHIN STORIES

A BANDETTE URCHIN STORY, STARRING FRECKLES IN...
WRITER: PAUL TOBIN
ARTIST: SARAH BURRINI
COLORIST: INES KORTH
NO BANDETTE
YOU HAVE A JOB, DEAR FRECKLES? WHAT DO YOU MEAN?
IS THIS ONE OF THOSE HORRIBLE THINGS WHERE YOU NEED TO WAKE UP IN THE MORNING?
CAN THIS BE TRUE?
YES. I'M STARTING TODAY AT LE MACARON SENSUELLE.
OHH! THE PASTRY STORE!

BUT... YOU MUST STEAL ME SOME ÉCLAIRS. BAGS OF PETIT FOURS! AND TARTS! YOU MUST THIEVE SOME TARTS!
I WILL DEVOUR ALL THE PAIN AU CHOCOLAT YOU CAN DELIVER! AND CHAUSSON AUX POMMES!
BANDETTE, I'M GOING TO WORK AT LE MACARON SENSUELLE. I WILL NOT STEAL.
I'M SORRY, BUT...

Le Macaron Sens
Chocolat
...YOU MAY NOT HAVE THEM.

ONE DAY LATER.
PASTRIES, MY DEAR FRECKLES, ARE MUSIC FOR THE STOMACH.

AND EVERYBODY LISTENS.

TWO DAYS LATER.
NO, BANDETTE.
PIFF.

THREE DAYS LATER.
NO, BANDETTE.
AHH! AHH!

FIVE DAYS LATER.
NO, BANDETTE.
SLAP
Pain
Croiss
Brioche

NINE DAYS LATER.
SLAP
NO, BANDETTE.

BUT THEN...
FRECKLES, MAY I TALK TO YOU FOR A MOMENT?
OH? IS... SOMETHING WRONG?
NO. NOT AT ALL.
I JUST NEED TO TELL YOU...

... I'VE SOLD THE STORE. A MYSTERIOUS STRANGER OFFERED ME... WELL... QUITE AN ALLURING SUM. I COULD NOT RESIST.
IT'S TIME FOR ME TO EXPLORE THE WORLD.
OH, YOU'RE LEAVING? DOES THIS MEAN... I'M OUT OF A JOB?

NO. THE NEW OWNER SPECIFICALLY REQUESTED THAT YOU STAY ON.
AS MANAGER, IN FACT. YOU'VE BEEN PROMOTED!
FARE-WELL, MISS MANAGER.

HMMM.

OH. I SEE. YOU?
OUI. OF COURSE. I SOLD A MESSY PICASSO THAT I'D DISCOVERED UPON A WALL, THEN PURCHASED THIS BOULANGERIE.
I COULD NOT LET MYSELF BE THWARTED.

AND NOW, SINCE THESE PASTRIES ARE MINE...

SMAKK!

NO, BANDETTE.
THOSE ARE FOR CUSTOMERS ONLY.
The End

MONSIEUR IN: Souvenirs
YEARS AGO. THE RIVIERA.
STORY AND ART BY COLLEEN COOVER

WELCOME TO HOTEL LUX, MISS KING.
THANKS! THREE DAYS OFF!
I'M GOING TO MAKE THE MOST OF IT!

THAT EVENING.

ALLOW ME.
LEON CORVID, AT YOUR SERVICE.
I'M VIOLET. VIOLET KING.

SOON.
SEVEN! MADEMOISELLE KING WINS AGAIN.
YES!
YOU'RE ON A LUCKY STREAK!

YOU MUST HAVE BROUGHT ME LUCK, LEON!
CARE TO JOIN ME FOR DINNER?
HMPH!
AS CHEAP AS HER COSTUME BEADS!

I'D BE DELIGHTED TO DINE WITH YOU, VIOLET.
IF I MAY SUGGEST A PLACE I KNOW, OF SUPERIOR QUALITY?

MMM, WONDERFUL! HOW DID YOU EVER FIND THIS PLACE?
THERE ARE MANY SUCH GEMS, IF YOU KNOW WHERE TO LOOK.
PERMIT ME TO SHARE THEM WITH YOU?

I HAVE TO GO BACK TO WORK TOMORROW.
I'LL MISS YOU, VIOLET.

BUT I SHALL ALWAYS TREASURE OUR TIME TOGETHER.

THE NEXT DAY.

My dear Violet—
Forgive my impudence.
I have kept your lovely beads
as a memento. Please accept
this poor substitute,
and remember your most
ardent admirer—

DON'T SPeaK Her NaMe

By Paul Tobin

Illustrations by Colleen Coover

Cole Norton loved to walk through his family tree during his nightly security routes at the museum. Step by step. Age by age. The Norton family archives reached back almost seven hundred years, back to the time of the Hundred Years' War and the Black Death. Cole had studied his own family extensively. They were ingrained in his mind. So when he walked through the aisles in of the darkened museum, patrolling his assigned routes as a security guard, he had a litany of dates at his disposal. His ancestor's birth years, in many cases. Their deaths as well. All of these dates matching up, in Cole's mind, with the paintings and the sculptures and the other works of art.

He passed a tapestry woven while his ancestors still lived in Genoa.

There was a Berthe Morisot painting on the wall that had originally been displayed in a photographer's former studio on the Boulevard des Capucines, hung there for an exhibition that opened on April the fifteenth of 1874, a group show by the Anonymous Society of Painters, who would soon become known as the Impressionists. While that painting was still hanging on that wall, Cole's great-great-great-grandfather was marrying into a banker's family and beginning the Norton family's transition into a moneyed sort of gentility, away from farming, shop-keeping, and the one scandalous enterprise into brothel ownership.

In one gallery was a Lucian Freud painting first shown in the museum on the week Cole had been absent to attend his mother's funeral.

A Fernando Botero sculpture had been acquired by the museum and placed on display the very day Cole's first son, Clement, had been born.

In a little alcove was a Maurice Utrillo painting of the street where Cole's great-great-grandfather Armand Norton had closed his front door and marched off to die in the first World War, painted at a time when Armand's footsteps had not even ceased to echo.

Cole waved to another of the security guards, Alice, as she walked past an Otto Dix painting created while Cole's great-grandfather was smuggling refugees out of Germany, a painting that was brought into the museum on the day Cole had taken his girlfriend Marie out for a night of dancing and drinking wine, and then found to his amazement that he was proposing to her, and that to his joy she was accepting.

"Quiet night," Alice said, shining her flashlight into the alcoves.

"Quiet night," Cole answered. Some nights they would speak at length. Other nights they would only nod. This was one of the nodding nights, it seemed. They both hesitated, and moved on. There were routes to walk. Doors to check. Security at the museum was very good. Museums are plagued by theft, of course, and precautions must be taken. The museum had the very latest technologies, but also the very oldest: plentiful guards.

Cole continued making his rounds. Only once did his night waver from the norm. He heard footsteps where there shouldn't have been any, but when Cole investigated it was just Hatty Hooks, another of the guards, making an emergency run to the nearest bathroom. She was four months pregnant. Cole couldn't help but wonder what art might arrive at the museum to coincide with the arrival of Hatty's first child.

"Can you watch my area too?" she asked Cole, hurrying past. It would only mean that he had to walk a little faster on the route. Hatty was posted in the Old Masters wing tonight, adjacent to Cole's route. He wouldn't have time to linger and his feet might ache if Hatty took too long, but that was of no consequence. This was family. The guards were family. And Hatty, of course, was creating her family even as Cole said, "No problem!" and waved her hurriedly on. She was making a child within her, after all, crafting with evolution's talents, a master far surpassing even the most talented of brush strokes.

Tonight, at least for the duration of Hatty's off-schedule bathroom break, Cole wouldn't have time to admire the actual brush strokes on any of the paintings. Once, in day's past, in years gone, he'd wanted to be a painter. Well, he supposed he was a painter. But only a hobbyist. One of the rooms in the apartment he shared with Marie was given over to his painting. Five easels. Three sitting chairs for models, such as his wife, and his sons, including Clement, who was now studying

One of the rooms in the apartment he shared with Marie was given over to his painting.

engineering in Belgium, and who had lived in the room for seventeen years.

On Mondays and Tuesdays, on what amounted to Cole's weekend, he would drive to the mountains and paint *"en plein air,"* as it was called, not only painting nature but experiencing it. He felt he could almost hear those paintings sing. Art, of course, must sing. Life must sing. On work days, he would paint before his shift at the museum, sometimes with Marie reading in one of the chairs, either modeling or simply keeping him company, alerting him to the time so that he wouldn't become so engrossed in his art that he'd miss the train to the museum. Other times she'd be cooking. Sometimes she'd be sleeping. Their schedules didn't exactly match. Cole treasured the times when he could paint his wife sleeping in the chairs. At other times when he painted he would have music playing or would be himself singing, but when his wife slept he kept the room as quiet as possible, engrossed in the soft sounds of his brush against the canvas, and the adorable snores of Marie.

By the time Hatty returned from the bathroom with an apologetic shrug and an explanatory pat on her stomach, Cole's legs had begun to ache from covering both areas, but it was a welcome ache. The ache of work well done. Hatty resumed her routes and Cole returned to his, alone. He spent the rest of his shift walking through the museum, matching the time periods of the various artworks with the history of his family, and studying the brush strokes of his favorite works. Nothing of any real consequence occurred.

It wasn't until he was home that he discovered the theft of the paintings.

• •

Marie was asleep on the couch when Cole arrived home. He stood watching her for some seconds, aware of his slightest noise. Then, he was off to the kitchen to see about having a slice of cake. Just yesterday his wife had made the most delicious strawberry cake. He'd had a few bites before leaving for work and she'd scolded him, which both of them had enjoyed. The cake was on the kitchen table, but was half eaten, now. Perhaps his youngest son, Marcus, had sniped a couple pieces during a visit? He was living on campus, now, but often came home to scrounge food and use the laundry room. It was sad to have missed him. Standing in the kitchen, contemplating his family, Cole became aware of a buzzing noise. It took him several moments to place it.

"My phone?" he said. He'd left it on a table in the living room. But who would be calling at this hour, nearly four in the morning? And more importantly, why? It would wake Marie. Cursing quietly, Cole strode into the living room, where his wife was sitting up on the couch, looking around in bleary incomprehension.

"What's that?" she murmured.

"Phone. Sorry. Go back to sleep so I can admire you."

"I'm think go to bed?" she said. Not her best sentence, but she was barely awake. Rising, wrapping a blanket around her, she started to walk past Cole toward the bedroom, but she stopped as she woke up enough to realize what was happening.

"So late?" she said as she looked to the phone Cole was grabbing. "What if it's . . ." Her voice trailed off. Cole knew what Marie was thinking. Every parents' worry. Their children. But the call was coming from work.

"Just work," he hurriedly told Marie while answering the phone.

"Work," she answered in an uncomplimentary voice. Marie wanted him to change jobs. She knew he loved the museum and the art, but she was tired of being alone at nights, and tired of the toll on his legs and feet, all those nights of walking those hard floors.

"Cole here," he said into the phone.

"Cole? Sorry to bug you. It's Hatty. I knew you'd be up. Could you cover my shift tomorrow? I'm a puke machine. Need a couple days."

"No problem," Cole answered, on automatic. He could feel his wife's gaze. They'd been planning on an apartment cleaning the next day. A thorough one. Cole looked at his wife, trying to decide if she was more irritated at him working yet another extra shift, or how he was avoiding the apartment cleaning. But he explained it was for Hatty, and Marie folded as Cole knew she would. The two were friends. Hatty often asked Marie for advice on her pregnancy.

Just yesterday his wife had made the most delicious strawberry cake.

Soon, Marie was in bed and had returned to her snoring. But the phone call had ruined Cole's chance of sleep for at least an hour, so he wandered into his painting studio.

And into disbelief.

"My paintings," he gasped.

They were gone.

Breathing as if he'd run the entire city's length, Cole stood in the room, willing his paintings to appear. But they were gone. Vanished. And the little Suzanne Valadon sketch he'd purchased from an auction house for an entire month's pay, also gone. He'd toiled for that Valadon sketch. He'd discussed the purchase with Marie, expecting and even somewhat wanting her to talk him out of it, but she'd been entirely in favor of the purchase. "You'll be inspired," she'd kept saying. "You'll always have a little fire in that room." The sketch was of a woman in her bath. One leg over the side. There was the suggestion of another presence in the room. Drawn in charcoal by the hand of a woman who'd posed for, and slept with, some of the greatest names of the Impressionist era. A woman who matched them in artistry. Cole had spent nights staring at that sketch on the wall, feeling as if Marie had been right, as if the sketch were a heat source. He'd used that fuel in his own paintings. He'd channeled that fire. He'd felt like he was a link in a chain that went back to Valadon, to Degas, to the Old Masters, and back through history older than his family reached.

But they were gone. Vanished.
But now that chain was shattered.

The wall was empty.

The sketch and his paintings were gone. The easels and the posing couches were empty. They seemed to accuse him, those empty chairs and easels.

"Maybe . . . Marie moved them?" He felt like he was grasping for any margin of balance and sanity.

"The camera!" he exclaimed. Of course. The camera. When Clement moved to Belgium, when Cole had transformed his son's old bedroom into a painting studio, Marie had often worried she would interrupt Cole in his work if she simply breezed into the room, snapping his artistic flow by wandering into the studio while he was in what she called his painting "madness." So she'd installed a camera. A way of watching Cole and the room from anywhere in the house, so she would know if she could play her music or the television at a decent volume, or wander into the room. Cole had never said it aloud, but he suspected his wife just enjoyed watching him in secret, just as he enjoyed watching her slumbering, or when he'd peek around a doorway and watch her curled on the couch, reading. But the important thing for now was that the camera would have a record of the night's events.

He raced from the studio and nearly pulled a drawer entirely out of a kitchen cabinet while searching for the proper cords. He had to wire the camera's feed to his laptop. Less than a minute later, the recording was beginning. Cole stared at the images of his studio. The room was untouched. The paintings were in place. Cole was looking into what he considered as a proper past, but he knew it wouldn't last. With the video on high speed he watched the shadows change. There were flickering lights as traffic passed by outside. As the seconds ticked away, Cole realized he was forgetting to breath.

Just as he gulped his first breath of air, a thief walked into the room.

A teenaged girl. In a bright costume and black mask.

"Bandette?" Cole gasped. Of course he recognized her. There were no museum guards in the whole of the city, the nation and perhaps even the world, who were not aware of the thief named Bandette. Locks seemed to mean nothing to her. The most expensive and complex security systems did not so much as slow her pace. Truth told, Cole had admired her in the past. She was a rogue. An artist, even, in her own way.

But now she was stealing from him.

His stomach twisting, Cole watched as the girl stood poised in front of his original Valadon sketch. She viewed it from several angles, some of them quite odd, such as standing on her hands, and once even perched atop an easel as if she were a weightless bird. Then, suddenly, the deed was done. The sketch was in her hands. She placed it on an easel and admired it there, the small sketch dwarfed by the wooden frame, looking small, and . . and . . .

"Helpless," Cole whispered.

And then the sketch was truly gone, tucked somehow into the girl's cape. Cole knew in that moment that he would likely never see his Valadon sketch again. He had no chance to say goodbye. There was only that one final glimpse. A bit of shadow disappearing into a red cloak. And then . . . gone.

And Bandette herself, seen in the video footage, was leaving. With an almost impossibly light grace, she was headed for the open door. But then she seemed to suddenly stop. And notice Cole's paintings. Despite the mask, he could make out her growing interest.

"No," Cole whispered. "Leave them alone. Just, please, leave them alone." But of course he knew she wouldn't. He knew he would watch Bandette steal his paintings. And that's exactly what he did. With his fingers tingling and his emotions raging, wanting to scream and to throw things, Cole Norton sat and watched the young thief steal painting after painting. She opened the windows and crawled outside with them, even leaping through the open window at times, even though they were on the third floor. There was little to aid climbing on the walls outside. A few pipes, perhaps. But the young thief was legendary. A pipe would be enough. It could hold her, and, sadly, the paintings. Years of work. All those memories in his paintings. Or, Bandette's paintings, now, Cole supposed.

When the paintings were gone, Cole thought the video would end. It was triggered by motion, after all. Certainly the next images would be of Cole himself walking into the studio, his shocked expression evident in the currently all-but-empty room. But, no. The footage skipped forward some five minutes and then there she was again. Bandette. But this time she had a plate. A fork. And a very generous slice of cake.

Cole swore. Loudly.

And then he watched as the young thief walked around the room, staring at . . . what? The empty places where his paintings had been? Was she gloating?

"Lovely!" came the voice from the video. Cole jumped and almost fell. He'd thought the tape was silent. There'd been no noise, before. None.

"Most delicious!" Bandette said. Her voice was full of amazement, slightly muffled by the cake in her mouth. She held the plate up to her eyes, studying the cake. "Astounding!" she said. "But, oh! *Non non non.* I must be sure. The jury of my stomach must pretend to be unconvinced!" Her fork worked at the cake and gathered a prodigious amount. "More evidence is then necessary, no?" Her mouth closed down. Abruptly, although the plate itself never seemed to move, Bandette executed a full roll, and then with a little hop she was sitting in the open window, watching the city at night and finishing the cake. There was no more noise. Everything was silent again. If Cole strained, he could her the traffic outside.

Soon, after only an eternity of torment, the video ended. The last Cole saw of Bandette was her walking out of the room, carrying the plate and the fork. Then, as if he were carrying an unthinkable weight on his back, Cole stood and walked into the kitchen. There, in the drying rack, was the plate. And the fork. Cleaned. And dry now.

Bandette had washed the dishes.

But stolen his paintings.

Cole Norton sat and watched the young thief steal painting after painting.

• • • • • • • • • • • • • • • • • • • •

Cole brought the oddly shaped whistle to his lips. He blew. It produced absolutely no sound, but he did notice two cats, languidly perched on the wide stone rail of nearby staircase, sit up straight and glare at him in annoyance.

Despite there being no noise, he put the whistle back in his pocket. He'd been strictly instructed to only blow it once. The whistle had arrived this afternoon in a small wooden puzzle box that Cole had spent almost twenty frustrating minutes to determine how to open. The box had been left on his studio windowsill after he'd used the friend of a friend, or more precisely the disreputable friend of a semi-reputable friend, to contact the mysterious man he was hoping to meet.

And now, four days after the theft of his beloved Valadon sketch and his life's work in art, Cole was waiting at three in the morning, in near total darkness, outside the Café Elemental, long after all the lights on the street had been extinguished. There was no neon glow from the café, no cars passing by, no lamps in the windows, not even the streetlights were shining, oddly. It was as if even they had surrendered to the accord of darkness. Only the moon was providing any illumination. His wife Marie had once told him that the moon plays witness to all deeds in the night, and that she's unwilling to miss the most interesting of the action, so she shines her flashlight down on humanity, observing everything, including our worst accomplishments and our best mistakes. Cole could remember Marie in his studio speaking her whimsical thoughts while she remained otherwise still. He'd been painting her portrait. It was gone, now. It was among the missing paintings. A tangible memory of his Marie had been ripped away.

"Cole Norton," he heard. He tried to suppress a jump and was not entirely successful. The voice had been low. A man's voice. But, from where? There was no one on the street. Cole's eyes darted to the windows, the doors, the darkened recesses, but there was no one. For a few ludicrous moments he even looked to the cats, wondering if they'd spoken. The strange night seemed full of lunacy.

"Cole Norton," the voice repeated. "Up here." Cole's gaze rose sharply to the rooftops, where a man stood on the roof of a four story building, leaned out over the void, holding a chimney for support, angled out over the ledge with no evident concern, his form outlined by the moon behind.

It was a man dressed entirely in black.

A thief who'd been known for decades.

A legend to equal Bandette's.

"Monsieur," Cole whispered.

"Yes," the man said, although Cole thought he'd spoken too low to be heard. Then, to Cole's shock, Monsieur released his grip on the chimney and fell forward. Cole gasped and scrambled backward, afraid the man would tumble onto him, but Monsieur grasped at the edge of a windowsill, which sent his body twisting to the right, to where he momentarily balanced his weight on a balcony and then released with a curving arc that sent him first to the café's awning and then lightly to the street, landing so softly that Cole heard not the slightest sound. Even the cats sat up straighter, impressed. Cole smiled and thought, yes, *yes;* this is the man who can do what needs to be done.

"Your note explained you've had a problem," Monsieur said. "The theft?" Even though the man was now standing in front of him, the blackness of his body suit seemed to absorb all evidence of his presence. It was as if Cole were talking to a tall, cold, shadow.

"Yes," Cole said, choking back his rage. "My paintings. Why would she take them? They're worthless to someone like her. She's destroyed my life for . . . what? Whimsy? The depraved thrill of stealing?"

"And you're certain it was Bandette?" Monsieur asked.

"Don't speak her name!" Cole spat out. "All this time, I found her amusing! A playful rogue! I was a fool. She's a monster. I can't even . . . I can't sleep. To think of what she's done! I look at my Marie and think of all the memories that were on those canvases! All the brush strokes I tried to make sing! All the time I spent feeling alive, my canvas in front of me, Marie laughing, singing, reading, the mountains and the forests around me! All of them, simply carried out the window by that thief! So, no, Monsieur. Do not speak her name. I won't hear it. Call her what she is. A monster."

For long moments, the street was entirely still. The man in front of Cole was silent. The cats, padding closer, made no noise. The moon's eager flash-light shown down on the street, with a cloud passing overhead, a shadow moving across the avenue as if some great underwater shark was lurking below. Cole was trying to suppress his emotions. He hadn't even understood the depths of his own rage until he'd spoken. He hadn't known there was so much anger, waiting just below the surface.

"And, for what you want me to do," Monsieur finally spoke, "what can you offer me in return?"

Cole wanted to say such things as "gratitude," or perhaps "the knowledge you have done the right thing," which to his mind was no small thing, but he knew that he was talking to yet another thief, perhaps not the monster of the girl who stole his life, but a thief nonetheless. And their kind must be paid.

"For the return of my paintings," Cole said, "I offer the Valadon sketch that was among what the monster took from me. You may keep that. But my paintings, my memories, I must have them back. Please, I must have them back."

Again, the street went silent. This time, though, Cole could almost hear the calculations in the man's brain. He could feel the presence of a decision being made.

"I am a fan of Valadon's work," Monsieur said. Cole remained silent, having heard the tone of the man's voice. Monsieur had been speaking of the factors in a decision, not speaking of the decision itself. Silence resumed. The moon was eager with her light. The cats came padding even closer.

"Bandette is my greatest rival," Monsieur finally said. "I will see what can be done." And with that spoken, he turned and walked away, striding with confidence to the nearest wall, which he scaled as if it were a simple staircase, up and up to the rooftops and the shadows, and then he was gone. The cats wandered away. The moon was still shining. Cole remained in the street.

"Don't speak her name, Monsieur," he found himself saying to the darkness. "Did you not hear what I asked? Do not speak her name."

• •

A week passed. And then, two. Cole would find little notes, hidden in odd places. He found them on his windowsills. He found them in the case for his glasses. One night, when he was walking his route at the museum, the beam of his flashlight began flickering so he took it apart to check on the batteries, only to find a note wrapped around the middle battery, written in a firm hand, entirely legible, addressed to him.

These notes were from Monsieur, reporting his progress. He'd tracked Bandette across a rooftop, but lost her. He'd seen her from afar, carrying something, witnessed only through a telescope as she raced across a wire high above the rooftops, then disappeared into darkness. Monsieur had set traps for Bandette at several places where he felt it was possible she would try to sell Cole's paintings, but she had not, at least yet, arrived. Two days later Monsieur had found one of Bandette's most secret lairs, but when he picked the lock and gained entry he'd found nothing but empty rooms and a single candy bar wrapper, upon which Bandette had drawn three passable cartoons of a horse in a hat. Monsieur had once even attended a party held by Bandette herself, celebrating the birthday of Bandette's dog, Pimento. Attendees at Bandette's parties were forbidden to talk business of any kind, but Monsieur had still taken the opportunity to snoop around for the Valadon sketch or Cole's paintings, but he'd found no evidence of either. Speaking with Bandette herself, Monsieur had lightheartedly asked if she'd had any interesting thefts of late. She'd said, "No."

Bandette had said, "No."

How that burned in Cole's stomach. She'd stolen his very life, and it was not even interesting to the monster. He wondered how many other lives she'd ruined. He wondered, too, if he'd picked the right man for the job to target Bandette and recover his paintings, because Monsieur seemed to be making no real progress. The man had even been ushered out of Bandette's party for talking too much about the life of thieves. Bandette had said, "We speak of a beloved dog, tonight, Monsieur! Not open windows and stolen paintings! Unless of course you have commissioned a painting of Pimento? You have not? What a shame! I could have placed it next to the pigeons, who are fond of my Pimento and coo whenever he is near."

With each passing day, Cole felt the possibility of recovering his paintings slipping away. The police were of even less help than Monsieur. He'd filed a report, but when he'd stated that Bandette had stolen his paintings, the detective had only stiffened and then gave Cole a sorrowful look and a sympathetic pat on his shoulder. Cole had half expected the man to hug him.

"Ah," the man had said. "What Bandette steals is like a sunken ship, my friend."

"Oh?" Cole had said. "What do you mean?"

The officer had made a fluttering motion with his hand, and then answered, "Like a sunken ship, those things that Bandette steals . . . they sail away, and they never come back."

Cole had stomped his way furiously out of the police station. They hadn't even cared to see the footage he'd taken. They'd had the look of beaten dogs. They'd given up. Cole would not give up. He would fight for his art. All of the paintings were dear to him, but those paintings of Marie and Clement and Marcus, in particular, were a part of the family legacy. He would not let them slip away so softly. All throughout history, one way or another, the Nortons were fighters. He would not fail. He would find the monster. He would find his paintings.

It was a man dressed entirely in black. A thief who'd been known for decades. A legend to equal Bandette's.

Marie was worried about him. The morning after the theft he'd showed her the footage. She'd been amazed, because Bandette must have walked past Marie, sleeping on the couch, several times.

"Bandette must be so quiet!" his wife had exclaimed.

"Don't speak her name," he'd answered. "Call her only by what she is. A monster. After what she's done, she does not deserve a name." Then, in an action he recognized even that morning as petty, he'd thrown out the remainder of the strawberry cake. What a useless gesture. But it had been satisfying, too. It had needed to be done.

"Hnn," Cole grunted, thinking of the memories, of Marie trying to calm him, of Monsieur leaving the useless notes. He found that he was grasping far too hard on his flashlight, walking through the wide dark halls of the museum in the depths of the night. He passed Alice, who wanted to talk about some foolish boy who'd been dating her daughter, but he had no time for such conversations. He passed by Hatty, who patted her stomach and waved at him, but he'd only given her a nod and moved on. He passed by countless paintings, hundreds of statues and other works of art, but barely noticed them. It was important to keep his feet moving. One foot after another. Finding balance. The night was too quiet. It did not intrude in his thoughts. But then, what could possibly intrude there in his mind? There was only enough room for his thoughts of the monster Bandette. Everything else would simply burn away.

"Ngh?" he grunted. There was something on the wall, a note affixed with a piece of tape, stuck to the wall beneath a painting by Jeanne Mammen. The painting was of two women dancing with two men, but the women were looking with great meaning to each other and the men were barely there, only suggestions of lines and paint, while both women were starkly realized. In days past, Cole would have considered how the painting had been created during the first stirrings of the second world war, at a time when the Norton family was divesting their banks of German investment. But now, Cole barely noticed the painting. He only cared about the note. It was from Monsieur.

"I've found her," the note said.

Ten steps down the hall, beneath an Albert Birkle painting, was another note.

"I believe I know where she is keeping your paintings," the new note read. Cole then discovered a following note of, "Would you like to come along?" beneath a George Grosz painting of two donkeys with a multitude of war machines and missiles strapped to their backs.

"Come along?" Cole said to himself, staring at the note. The bottom of the note had two square boxes. One marked "Yes." The other marked "No."

"Come along?" Cole said again, somewhat dazed if he was honest with himself. He took a single step and heard something skittering along the floor. Startled, he looked down to see that he had kicked a pen. Still startled, he picked up the pen and looked around. Where was Monsieur hiding? Why do thieves need to play such games?

Cole marked the "Yes" box and then stood dumbly. What to do now? His life was in balance and the tall cold man was leaving notes like some mischievous grade school child. Having no other idea of what to do, Cole returned the note to the wall where he'd found it, deciding to post it there and then walk away to a vantage point where he could observe it from afar. But when he turned around, he almost screamed, and in fact did gasp, at a volume that was nearly a shriek.

There was a balloon floating down the hall.

It wafted slowly, like a ghost.

It was yellow, catching the occasional moonbeams allowed access into the museum from the windows so high on the walls. There was something written on the balloon, written in a pen that made the letters glow in the darkness.

An address.

A time.

A . . . dress code?

Cole stood dumbly until the balloon bounced off his chest.

. . . .

Two nights later, Cole was dressed in his best suit but standing in a back alley, trying to avoid stepping in any of the puddles from the recent rain, and especially any of the puddles that did not look like rainwater at all.

"And, why have you brought us here?" Marie asked. She was dressed in her finest skirt, the light green one with the delicate embroidery of a landscape at the hem. Her silk blouse gleamed in the flickering lights, and her cardigan kept her warm. She was perched atop a wooden palette, the remnant of some shipment, in order to keep her best boots dry.

"Monsieur's note said to be here," Cole told her. He was feeling ridiculous. What had he gotten himself into? More importantly, what had he gotten Marie into? But Monsieur's note had stressed that it was safe, and that Marie would need to be there, and that they must dress nicely, as they would have to navigate their way through some sort of secret ball, some gathering of the city's more illicit and yet prosperous citizens.

"To the back rooms," Cole said, not talking to Marie, not talking to himself, perhaps talking only to a balloon that he had deflated and put in his pocket that night at the museum, taking it home with him and blowing it up in his empty studio while Marie was sleeping on the couch. The balloon had explained, with its softly glowing letters, that they would make their way through the party, and through a secret door to the back rooms. Cole could remember reading the words again and again, finally dropping the balloon to drift along the increasingly dusty floor of his studio. The balloon had originally held helium and been able to float, but that night it had only his breath. It still should have floated. It should have soared. Hot air rises, after all, and since the day of the theft, every bit of Cole . . . including his breath . . . had felt as if it were burning. He could not wait to confront Bandette. He could not wait to reveal himself. Perhaps he would be the one to catch her and bring her to justice at last. She would spend years in prison to pay for her horrible crimes.

"Monsieur should be here soon," Cole told his wife. "Then this will all begin. Then this will all end."

"Do the paintings truly mean that much to you?" Marie asked. She was looking deep into his eyes. It made him feel exposed.

"Yes," he told her, without hesitation. "Yes. They are my life. They are my memories of you. Of our sons. Of . . . I'm not sure how to say this. They are my memories of my very existence. They are how I sing to this world." His wife stepped off the wooden palette and looked even deeper in his eyes. Her face was half in shadow. He wondered if Monsieur was watching them, in secret. He wondered what Marie was looking for, searching so deep in his eyes. Whatever it was, she found it. She gave a nod. A smile.

"If that is truly what you believe," she said, "then we are doing the right thing." Cole was amazed by the look in her eyes. The ferocity. He could remember the first time he'd ever seen Marie, sitting in a café one table away from him. He'd been on a first date. She'd been his date's surreptitious friend, there to help if he turned out to be a wretch. The date had not gone well, but only because he could not take his eyes off Marie. Two days later, she had called him. They had been together ever since. He adored the way she would stomp her feet to make a point. The way she would mix cinnamon and honey on her toast. The softness of her snores. The vulgarity of her jokes. The way she would draw little cartoons of herself that he would often find when he came home from the museum at nights, notes left there for him to see, little reminders that even though she was asleep, he was not alone. There were countless other things about this woman that made him happy, and most were indescribable. Simply put, she made him feel, inside, as if he were singing.

"It's good to see you smile again," she said. "What are you thinking about?"

"I'm thinking that, with you at my side, I don't need some thief in a black bodysuit. We can do this alone." With that, he strode forward to a door. It was the only one in the back alley with a working light overhead, and Cole suspected it must be the door where they were supposed to go. His suspicions were strengthened when he reached for the doorknob and noticed a recent marker drawing of a balloon on the door itself, illustrated with an arrow pointing to the doorknob.

"There?" Marie said, gesturing to the door.

"Here. I'm sure of it."

"But are you sure we can do this, alone, together?"

"Of course. No matter what, I'll find a way. A Norton always finds a way. And if I'm with you, I'm unstoppable."

But when he opened the door, and found what was there, just inside, it stopped him cold.

• • • • • • • • • • • • • • • • • • • •

It was a pig.

A young one. Barely larger than a bread loaf.

"A pig?" Cole found himself saying, speaking as if pigs were mythical creatures unimaginable to encounter in real life.

"A pig?" Marie echoed, with the same disbelief in her voice. Cole looked up from the pig to the rest of the room, which was cast in darkness, a darkness that he barely registered before a figure stepped from the shadows.

It was a teenage girl. Wearing a mask. Dressed in a green matador outfit with gold trimmings.

"Ah, Pietro, you scamp!" she said, gathering the pig into her hands.

"Matadori?" Cole whispered.

"The same!" she said, brightening. "You have heard of my deeds, then? My mastery of the sword?" She produced a fencing sword with a wicked tip. It flashed in the darkness, moving so quickly that it could barely be seen, producing sounds like the crack of a whip.

Of course Cole had heard of Matadori, and even seen some few pictures. She was a rival of Bandette. And a friend as well. They seemed to be both. But this girl who stood before him was a known assassin. A deadly killer. Which meant . . .

"A trap," Cole said, moving in front of Marie. Then, he struck out at the killer. If this was his end, his ancestors would know that Cole Norton died fighting.

"Pigs are inquisitive, you know, and my Pietro is the most curious pig of all."

His punch missed. The young girl stepped to one side and he almost toppled over. But instead he used his momentum and spun around, trying to knock her senseless with an elbow. But she simply wasn't where she was supposed to be. Cole spun himself in a full circle.

"Where?" he asked, fury and rage fueling him.

"He eats carrots and peas," Matadori was telling Marie, holding up the pig to show her. She'd put her sword away, as if to say that against a fighter as weak as Cole, she didn't need it, mocking him.

He grabbed for her neck from behind, but she ducked low and took a step back, dodging his grasp and ending up behind him.

"But these vegetables, they make my Pietro crazy!" she told Marie. "He romps and runs. Pigs are inquisitive, you know, and my Pietro is the most curious pig of all." Cole kicked out behind him, like a horse. The blow would send the girl flying. But instead she was somehow in front of him again, once more holding up the pig for Marie to see.

"Bandette believes my Pietro should wear a bowtie," she told Marie. "I do not. I would consider your advice in this matter." Cole attempted to tackle the assassin. She was so close and so small that she couldn't possibly avoid him. He leapt through the air and then somehow found himself outside, in the alley, about to roll into one of the unsavory puddles.

"Why are you leaping about in such a manner?" Matadori asked him. "Is this some modern dance?" She reached out and grabbed his collar, jerking him to a stop before he could splash into the puddle. He swept out a leg, which she skipped over with ease, turning in mid-air so that she could land lightly and walk back into the building.

"Are you coming?" she asked, holding the door. "Or do you wish to display more of your unusual dancing?"

"You're a killer!" he yelled.

"Ah, yes," Matadori said, admitting the truth of it while petting her pig.

"Sent her to kill us! To murder us! Sent by that thief!"

"Bandette?" Matadori said in a quizzical manner.

"Don't speak her name! But, yes! She needs to cover up her crime! She's a monster! And now you've been sent here to—"

"I have not been 'sent.' I have arrived. There was an invitation." The young girl paused and added, "There was said to be cake." Her voice was meaningful. Her gaze turned from Cole and settled on . . . Marie?

His wife took a deep breath. She did not seem to be afraid, but rather . . . resolved? Marie's eyes flickered away from the young girl and met Cole's. She gave him a smile that he couldn't understand and then turned to Matadori, to one of the most deadly assassins on the entire planet, the girl with a pig.

"Yes," his wife told the assassin. "There is cake."

• •

The next few moments were a blur to Cole. He could not understand what was happening. He was barely aware of being handed a pig, for one thing. It squirmed in his hands for some moments, but then Matadori showed him the proper method for holding a pig, which, she told him, is somewhat different than that of holding a baby, and more properly aligned with holding a ten pound bag of rice.

"Plus there is some drool," she admitted.

Matadori's sword flickered out, drawn and sheathed so quickly that Cole could barely register. But instead of murdering Cole, as he'd feared, she was only turning on the lights. They were in a storeroom of some sort. A . . . framing shop?

"This way," Matadori said, gesturing to a door. Marie came up next to Cole and took his arm. For some reason Cole felt he'd fallen into some strange wedding procession, except instead of him being the groom, he was the bride, and not carrying flowers but instead a small swine that had settled peacefully into his hands and was busily gnawing on his cuffs.

And then he was through the door and into . . . a gallery?

With paintings on the wall.

His paintings.

His paintings were on the walls.

And all around, a crowd was milling about, having drinks, conversing, talking, discussing the paintings. The gallery was brightly lit. There was music playing. The floors were of finely polished wood, matching the wooden columns that supported a ceiling with exposed rafters made of more polished wood.

Cole barely had time to register before the crowd parted, and there was Bandette.

"Ahh! Everyone!" she exclaimed. "The artist has arrived." She was twenty feet away. A somersault, and a cartwheel, and she had reached him. The hand of the monster was on his shoulder.

"May I present," she said, calling out to the attentive crowd, "Cole Norton! It is he who made these fine paintings! I believe now is a perfect time to applaud!" There was a pause, and then the crowd burst into applause.

"You stole my paintings!" Cole told Bandette. He meant to roar in rage, but was too confused by the gallery, the pig in his hands, the crowd, and the applause. "You stole my life at whim!"

"But no!" the monster told him. "At whim? I never do things at whim, except when the whim strikes me, which I now admit is often. But this time I, Bandette, the greatest thief in all the world, am innocent! Except for the part about stealing your paintings, if you count that." She looked at Cole. Her eyebrow raised in question. He did not know what to say.

"Do you count that?" she prompted.

"I do!"

"Ah. Guilty, then. But I did not steal at whim. I stole for a purpose. I stole by request."

"What? But . . . who? Who would ask you to steal my paintings?" The surrounding crowd was silent, watching this drama play out. Cole was intensely aware of them. Their gaze. Their rich suits. Their fancy dresses. The wine and the cocktails in their hands. The glints of jewelry from the diamonds and emeralds in bracelets and brooches, the rubies and sapphires in their necklaces and rings. The fine perfumes and rich colognes.

There was silence. Cole was almost trembling. Who could have hired the thief to steal the paintings? He expected the crowd to part and the mastermind to be revealed, and so it took him some time to understand that his wife, Marie, had raised her hand.

He stared at her in a stupefied manner.

"Marie?" he asked. She tried to answer, but her lips only trembled.

"I will take the podium!" Bandette announced. Then she looked around, frowned, and said, "Ah, but there is no podium. I must have taken it somewhere else. No matter, I can explain. Would you like a candy bar?"

The girl was offering him a candy bar. Holding it out.

"N-no," Cole said, looking between the thief and his wife.

"Wise man," Bandette said, putting away the candy bar in a hidden pocket of her cape. "Save room for cake. Our stomachs are not without limit."

"Why did you steal my paintings?" Cole managed to mutter. He wasn't sure if he was talking to Bandette or his wife. His eyes kept flickering to the walls, to where his paintings were hung in grand frames. What if he were to grab one or two of them and run? Would the crowds stop him?

"One night," Bandette said, doing to a cartwheel that ended beneath a table, "I was doing what many innocent people do. Climbing walls and peeking in windows. It was then that I saw a lovely sketch by Suzanne Valadon, an artist I treasure on account of her story, her art, and the many interesting vowel combinations in her name." Bandette's voice came from below the table, as did her hands, and then suddenly she flipped out from beneath and was standing on the table, straddling, Cole noticed, a cake.

"I slipped inside the room and was borrowing the art, much as one borrows a book from a library. It is very similar, yes?" Bandette looked to Matadori. The assassin shook her head.

"*Theoretically* similar," Bandette said, turning back to Cole. "I would have returned the Valadon, as I could see it was much loved, and I never wish to interrupt any *affaires d'amour*. What a wretch I would be!" Bandette again looked to Matadori. This time, the assassin nodded.

"But then, as I was leaving, I noticed where I was. It was as if I had fallen into a gold mine, or one of those splendid caves full of pirate treasure you read about and dream of finding, although it has only happened to me no more than anyone else. Four or five times." Bandette looked to the pig in Cole's hands for confirmation of this being normal. The pig squealed in response. Bandette nodded.

"I knew at once," Bandette said, "that others must see what I saw. These paintings." She gestured to the paintings on the walls. "How could they be cooped away? In that room, I must say, the paintings were silent. I needed to move them to where they could sing!"

"What?" Cole said. He felt staggered. Matadori reached out and took the pig from his hands, setting the swine on the floor.

"At whim? I never do things at whim, except when the whim strikes me, which I now admit is often. But this time I, Bandette, the greatest thief in all the world, am innocent! Except for the part about stealing your paintings, if you count that."

"I discovered a slumbering woman," Bandette announced, pointing to Marie. Then, speaking as an aside, the girl added, "She sleeps at night, it seems."

"Many people do, Bandette," Matadori told her.

"Oh? Most odd. But I am not here to judge others. Only art. And I was much moved, Cole Norton. Much moved. I woke your wife and asked if she were the artist. She informed me it was you. I inquired as to the galleries where you have shown your art, and she said . . . none!" The girl paused. Her chest heaved. She looked to the crowd. "Can you believe this?" she asked of them. "None!" The crowd shook their heads sadly.

"I should speak," Marie said. "He should hear this from me." Cole turned his gaze to his wife, still trying to process everything. To understand anything.

"I told Bandette that you always wanted to be an artist, but instead focused your love on me. On Clement and Marcus. On our family. I told her of how you sing while you paint. I told her of how you work at the museum and admire the brush strokes of the masters, but are unaware of how you yourself are a master."

"It is true," Bandette said, hanging upside down and entirely unconcerned from a rafter, held in place by one foot hooked over the edge. "I admire your art! I believe the others do as well." There were murmurs of assent and even some shouts of "genius" from the crowd. Cole's chest swelled.

Marie said, "But I also told Bandette that you'd given up on your dreams of being an artist, that you walk miles every night through other peoples' art, but are afraid to take the first steps for your own."

"So we needed a plan," Bandette said. "A plan where you would see how much passion you have for your art! How much fire there is within you! A plan that would remind you of how you treasure these paintings! Would you like to know what the plan was?"

"I think—"

"I decided to steal the paintings and hold a gallery show!" Bandette blurted. "Thereby allowing many of my friends to see the way your paintings can move the heart and inspire the mind! Oh, but, I have spoiled the secret of our plan. Have I spoiled the secret of our plan?" Bandette looked to Marie, who nodded, and Matadori, who shrugged, and to Pietro, who squealed.

"Unanimous, then," Bandette said. "I may as well reveal all. My friends are connoisseurs, you see. And I believe some of them would like to commission various portraits, the prices for such will begin at twenty thousand dollars."

"Commission . . . portraits?" Cole asked. He looked to the crowd. Several hands went up. A babble of voices. People were asking him to paint their wives. Their husbands. Their lovers. Their entire families. Even their pets. Several voices were offering prices much higher than even the astounding number Bandette had mentioned. Marie's hand came out to hold his, clenching fiercely.

"I'm sorry to have done it this way," his wife said. "But you needed a push. I could not have you walking the rest of your life away in hallways full of other peoples' dreams."

Cole looked to her. There were tears in her eyes. Her beautiful eyes. Her mouth was trembling. She was afraid he would be angry. She was afraid she had taken a chance, and lost. Cole's chest was full of fire, but it was fine. It was a good fire. He was thinking back to the first time he'd ever seen Marie. He was thinking back to when she, not he, had made that first call. If she hadn't phoned, if she hadn't taken a chance, he might never have held her hand, the way he was doing right now. Such a loss was unthinkable. Cole felt like he was now on the verge of another chance. This time, the leap . . . at least in part . . . would be his.

"Thank you," he told his wife, and watched the smile blossom on her lips.

"Look away!" Bandette instructed the crowd. "They are about to kiss! Please admire the paintings for some time." Marie laughed at Bandette, but Cole had no time for laughing. Yes; he was going to kiss his wife. He did it for some time, and would have done it longer but Marie demanded he meet with the people who were about to change his life, the ones hiring him for portraits and making outrageous offers concerning the paintings on the walls. He soon found himself shaking hands, talking of painting techniques with the surprisingly intelligent crowd, accepting commissions and promising to arrive at various mansions and even a castle, there to meet the subjects of the portraits.

It wasn't for several minutes that Cole realized that there was, there had to be, a price to pay. His wife had hired Bandette. *Hired* her. They had little money to spare. So then . . . the paintings? It was all he had of worth, and, as he knew, thieves must be paid.

"To the left down the hall," Bandette said. She was suddenly at his side.

"What . . . what is down the hall?" What game was she playing now? Is this how the price was to be paid?

"The bathrooms," Bandette said. "I have noticed your sudden expressions. Have you eaten too few candy bars? Such a thing always upsets my stomach."

"Oh. No. It's just that . . . I know for all you've done, there's a price."

"Ah. Yes. Indeed. And I'm afraid the price is quite steep." The girl's brows furrowed.

"Whatever it is, I'll have you know that—"

"Whatever it is? But, I thought you knew!

The price has been paid."

"My . . . paintings?"

"Your paintings?" Bandette said in an outraged voice. "*Non non non*! They are as you say! Yours! Do you think me a thief?"

"Well, yes?"

"Perceptive, I admit. But I would not steal your paintings. I have stolen other art, instead."

"Ah. The Valadon." Though it made him sad, the loss of his beloved Valadon was an acceptable price to pay. He'd offered it to Monsieur, after all.

"No need for that," Bandette said, taking his hand, leading him to a door, which she opened. It was a small closet holding two items of note. The first was an amazing full painting by Suzanne Valadon, leaned against a wall. Bandette reached in and then held up proudly, showing it to Cole.

"You see?" she said. "I've no need for your Valadon, as I have this one."

Cole cleared his throat and said, "But, wasn't that hanging at the Musee D'Orsay?"

Bandette shrugged and said, "Oh? Perhaps this is true. I forget where I acquired it." She slid the painting back into the closet, leaning it against the wall opposite the second of the interesting things in the closet. It was Monsieur. Bound and gagged. Somewhat squirming.

"And, him?" Cole asked.

"Monsieur. A fellow thief. I believe you have met?"

"I, um, hired him to find you. He's been on the search, leaving me notes about his progress. He left me notes at the museum that led me here to . . . to . . . " Cole stopped because of the way the young thief was looking at him. There was a certain whimsy to her smile that took him a moment to understand.

"Oh," he said. "The museum notes? The balloon? *You* left them?"

"It is true. Your attendance here was necessary, of course, so I decided to take the opportunity to lure you. It was a simple matter. I was at the museum anyway. I often visit at night."

"You . . . do? No. Don't tell me. But, why is Monsieur tied up?"

"A precaution, only," the girl said. "I feared he would steal what I have worked so hard to attain, even though, as they say, you can always trust a thief."

"It's . . . most commonly said that you, uh, *can't* trust a thief?"

"Is this true? How odd! But Monsieur is a good friend and a wise rival. And were he to walk off with the prize I have won . . . ? Oh, how my cheeks would flush! I would rage. I would have no recourse but to stomp on the floor and speak many words of harsh nature!" Cole watched the young thief, his current happiness growing into worry. He thought of all the treasures she'd stolen over the years, and his stomach roiled at how he had somehow already paid a price that could impress her. A price that Marie had promised. Years of servitude, then, for him? Or, worse, Marie?

"Please," he said, looking off to where Marie was talking to Matadori, discussing a painting on the wall, and looking to all the other guests milling about, laughing, with his artist's mind remembering their faces and preparing for the day he would paint their portraits, a life he would lead as an artist, no more long nights of walking alone without Marie, a life that could be his, but could also be destroyed if he couldn't conscience the price Bandette demanded.

"Please?" she said.

"Please, tell me the price for what you have done?"

"But, you do not know? Did you not watch the footage I provided after spotting your clever recording device in the studio? You saw me extracting the price I demanded!"

"I . . . did?" Cole's mind worked over the revelation that Bandette had known she was being filmed, and more furiously he thought about what she had taken? What was the price? The paintings she had stolen? The Valadon? But she'd promised they were still his? And the only other thing was . . . was . . .

"The cake?" he whispered, barely aloud, speaking to himself. And then, louder, "The cake?"

"But of course!" the thief said. "It was most astounding." She paused, as if considering something else, and then made him lean closer with a wave of her hand.

"I do not say this lightly, and I hope you take no offense, but I must honor the truth. Your wife, my friend, those cakes! It is she who is the greatest artist in your family!" With that spoken, Bandette began to walk off, but she stopped. The young thief paused. She waved Cole closer again.

"That night, in your apartment," she said. "I could not only see the fire in your brush strokes, but the fire of love you hold for your family. It is grand, that fire! It is the pinnacle of art. I decided then and there to give tribute to that love. I wanted you to be with your family. The five of you, together. You, your wife, your sons Clement and Marcus, and your art. It is a good family, and you do it honor. And now, I can wait no longer. My stomach, you understand, is impatient. Cake awaits. I would be a fool not to answer."

She strode off. A cartwheel was involved. As was a somersault and one bout of scurrying about on the floor and oinking in the fashion of the little pig, which she chased about. Soon, though, the girl had reached the table with the cake. Soon, she had sliced off a generous, and some might even say enormous slice of cake. After a few bites she began serving cake to the others as well. Matadori threatened several people with her sword, fending them off until she had a slice of her own. Then, as Cole watched the young thief sitting on the table, handing out slices of cake, Marie came to joined him. She smiled at him. He could not believe that any brush stroke would ever equal that smile. His wife took his hand and it was even better.

"What were you and Bandette talking about?" she asked.

"Don't speak her name," he said to his wife. "Never say that girl's name in my presence."

He turned to her and added, "Instead, you should sing it."

"Thank you," he told his wife, and watched the smile blossom on her lips.

WHAT'S BANDETTE STOLEN *NOW*?

By Colleen Coover

The one object central to the adventure of *The Six Finger Secret* is, of course, "The Artist's Studio" by Pierre Subleyras, a French artist based in Rome in the 18th century. Painted around 1747-1749, "The Artist's Studio" does *not*, to our knowledge, conceal a trove of coded messages secreted by legions of artists throughout the past three centuries. However, it does portray at least three images of the artist himself, as well as many faithful recreations of Subleyras' important previous works, including the large canvas which dominates the scene: "The Duke of Saint Aignan Investing the Prince of Cantalupe and Duke of Selci, with the Insignia of a Knight of the Holy Spirit," which also features paintings of paintings. Your faithful chronicler finds this to be delightful, or she did until it was time to draw the paintings in a painting of a painting in the pages of the volume you hold, at which time she determined that it was completely bonkers. Pierre Subleyras died in 1749, not long after "The Artist's Studio" would have been completed, having recently suffered from exhaustion due to overwork. No kidding!

The Artist's Studio by Colleen Coover

The Artist's Studio

Self-portrait of Pierre Subleyras. This self portrait of the artist Pierre Subleyras is on the reverse of "The Artist's Studio."

"The Artist's Studio," also referred to as "The Studio of the Painter," represents Pierre Subleyras's studio in Rome. In this painting he has depicted himself three times—he sits on a low stool on the bottom left and holds up a second self-portrait showing him as a young man, and the figure shown from back at the easel is also the painter. Hung on the walls and supported on easels there are twenty-five paintings interspersed with small-scale plaster casts of significant artworks on pedestals and pieces of furniture. These include the paintings "Crucifixion of Saint Peter," "The Mass of Saint Basil," "Portrait of Pope Benedictus XIV," and "Portrait of Virginia Parker Hunt," all by Subleyras as well. A fourth self-portrait was discovered on the reverse of "The Artist's Studio" in 1968 (seen above).

The Duke of Saint Aignan Investing in the Prince of Cantalupe and Duke of Selci, with the Insignia of a Knight of the Holy Spirit

SPECIAL THANKS

Paul

Special thanks to all those who helped keep us safe during the pandemic, at all levels. And a shout-out to some of my favorite writing spots–such as the Rocking Frog and Floyds–that are no more, unable to remain in business due to the financial strains of 2020, aka the Big No-Good Stupid Year. A huge cheer to the Circuit Bouldering Gym, which helped keep Colleen and I nearly almost sane during the past year. A big "thanks" to those who wore masks, and a glaring eye to those who didn't. A rousing cheer to those who create music, or comics, or games, or television and film and books and paintings and so much more: it's all a breath of fresh air to the soul. A cheer, also, to all the dogs I couldn't pet in 2020, and all the friends I couldn't see. Thanks to Shantel LaRocque and Brett Israel and everyone else at Dark Horse Comics, for all that you've done, and continue to do, with helping bring *Bandette* to the shelves. And a special thanks to my mom for sending Colleen and I all that cheese. I'm afraid your son ate most of it, giving very little to his wife, the woman he loves.

Colleen

Special thanks to Chris Roberson, Alison Baker, Shantel LaRocque, Brett Israel, Pierre Subleyras, Audrey Hepburn, Audrey Tautou, Katharine Hepburn, Henry Fonda, Marlene Dietrich, Ennio Morricone, Josephine Baker, Veronica Lake, Suzanne Valadon, James Coburn, Henri de Toulouse-Lautrec, Cary Grant, Hayao Miyazaki, Peter O'Toole, Joseph Pujol (just because), René Goscinny, Albert Uderzo, Hergé, Jacques Tardi, Rumiko Takahashi, and always: Paul.

about the authors

Paul Tobin is a writer in Portland, Oregon, working in a wide variety of genres. In addition to *Bandette*, he also writes all of the *Plants vs. Zombies* graphic novels, and co-writes *Wrassle Castle* with his wife, Colleen Coover. He has written horror, such as the Eisner-nominated *Colder*, and space adventure, such as *Heist* and *Eath Boy*, and fantasy stories such as his *Messenger* Webtoon, as well as *Mystery Girl*. He also works on media properties such as *Witcher*, *Aliens*, and has written most of the major Marvel and DC heroes. In addition to comics, Paul writes novels such as *Prepare To Die!*, and the middle grade *Genius Factor* series. He enjoys indoor rock-climbing and naps, but not at the same time.

Colleen Coover, co-creator of *Bandette*, is an illustrator living in Portland, Oregon. Her other works include the acclaimed comic for adults, *Small Favors*; the all-age-appropriate *Banana Sunday*; and the original graphic novel *Gingerbread Girl*. With Paul Tobin, she co-writes a fantasy adventure comic for middle readers: *Wrassle Castle*, drawn by the artist Galaad. When she is not drawing *Bandette*, Colleen enjoys indoor boulder climbing and indulging her passion for yarn-based handicrafts.